Ariadne Breylard

WINTER KNIGHTS DREAM

Editing by Madison Silvers

Proofing by Nina Fiegl

Cover art by Efa

Formatting by NVPLLC

Published by © Night Vision Publishing LLC (C1319203)

ISBN: PB: 978-1-963336-02-3

ISBN: 978-1-963336-19-1

Introduction

This Adult Fantasy Romance series is intended for mature audiences and is not suitable for young readers. The characters engage in multiple partner relationships and experience fated mates dynamics (why-choose). These relationships are inclusive, exploring diverse partnerships, including those of the same sex.

If themes such as LGBTQ+, multiple partners, open relationships, or poly are discomforting, it's advised to avoid this book series.

Themes and tropes in this book include: bonded, bullying, cliffhanger, enemies to lovers, fated mates, inst-love, love triangle, multiple POV, other-women-drama, second chance, secret identity, slow burn, smut/sexually graphic scenes with explicit language & description, soulmates, and steamy/suggestive scenes, unrequited love.

This book will end on a cliffhanger.

Ariadne Breylard

Winter

Knights Dream

To the Darkness
for allowing me to see the stars.

Contents

Chapter One

I struggled to breathe.

"Please, my love," the massive male before me begged. "Don't keep me in suspense. My name is Vale, and I'm yours forever if you'll have me."

Vale's eyes practically glowed from within. They were a vivid green, sparkling like gemstones in the sun. His skin was warm with a sun-kissed glow, and his hair was a shimmering ash blond with dark undertones that fell in soft, tousled waves around his broad shoulders. Vale's boxy features gave him a rugged, masculine appearance that accentuated his chiseled jawline and high cheekbones. His full lips curved into a gentle smile, exuding an open and inviting presence.

My eyes swam at his words. "You want me?"

It was a silly thing to say to your mate when meeting him for the first time, but I'd been rejected once before, and the experience had scarred me.

Vale's features softened, and a gentle smile tugged at his pink lips. "I've never wanted anything or anyone more in my entire life. Of course I want you. I want you right now, forever and always, my sweet mate. Please, tell me your name so I may kiss your perfect lips."

A tear slipped down my cheek, and my heart raced in my chest. But I accepted him—Vale, my mate.

"Lyra," I whispered. "My name is Lyra."

Vale lowered his face and murmured over my lips, "Beautiful, sweet mate. Please accept me."

"I do."

The words were barely out when he crushed his mouth to mine. He groaned at the contact, and I tentatively touched his chest. He wanted me, and we'd accepted the initial bond, but I was still shy.

Vale wrapped one hand around my shoulder, and the other curved over my ass as he bent and lifted me against his chest. I squeaked in surprise and felt him smile against my mouth, but he didn't release me. Instead, he encouraged me to wrap my arms and legs around his huge body.

"That's better," he hummed before retaking control.

His tongue was hot and determined as he swept it against mine, and he groaned with pleasure as I settled against him, returning his enthusiasm. There was loud chatter around us, and I remembered we weren't alone. I pulled away from him and looked into his eyes. He smiled and adjusted his hold to brush his thumb over my swollen lips.

"Hi."

"Hi," I replied, my voice trembling with disbelief and excitement.

Looking him over, I noticed his shirt for the first time.

My mouth fell open. "You're a Hornet?"

He was wearing a jersey from High Crest Academy, and based on his size, I guessed he was a Stopper.

"I am." His deep voice rumbled against my body. "And it looks like you're a long-time Shadows fan. But that's okay. I'll win you over to my team." He grinned, then pecked my lips again.

"What have ya got here, Vale?" A lithe male, who was also wearing a Hornets jersey, came up beside us. "Or are you in the habit of swooping up fans of the opposing team and kissing them senseless in front of a crowd?"

"You know I'm not, asshole." Vale playfully glared at his buddy.

"No, I know you're not." He patted Vale on the back and then looked at me. "Has the goddess blessed you in front of all these witnesses?"

Vale's beaming smile said it all, but he couldn't contain his excitement and let out a loud whoop. "Yes! Lyra is my mate!" he shouted, and the entire group erupted into thunderous cheers and applause.

As the crowd celebrated, the weight of Vale's words hit me and I realized the magnitude of what had happened. Had I really found one of my mates at a school party?

"This is my captain, Chet," Vale told me of his teammate.

"It's an honor to meet you," Chet said.

"It's nice to meet you, Chet." I shook his hand, which was a little awkward since Vale was still holding me. My legs were around his waist, and my other arm was around his shoulders.

"Holy shit, Lyra!" Callie squealed. "Is this real?"

I looked down at her and then back up to Vale. "Yes, it's real."

"You're damn right it is." He hugged me tight and kissed me again before setting me down. "I'm Vale." He tipped his head to Callie but didn't make any move to shake her hand. He simply tucked me against him and kept his arm around my shoulders.

"I'm Callie. Lyra's bestie." She winked at me and turned. "This is Jed, Brev, and Sidric," she said, pointing to the others of our group. Then she waved at my brother and his mate. "And these are our captains, Puck and Roko."

Vale reached out to each male and shook their hands. "Nice to meet you."

"And you." Puck eyed him cautiously, but Roko was clearly happy.

Jed and Brev shook his hand, and while I was conflicted about Sidric, he surprised me. "It's an honor to meet you. Lyra is dear to me. I look forward to you proving yourself to her. She deserves the best."

Vale's arm tensed around me as they stared each other down, but Vale gave him a nod. "I'll spend my days proving myself to her. I'm glad she's had such loyal people in her life. I'm not a jealous male, but let me be clear that she is my mate now and you are only her friend."

Sidric's lips lifted in a wide smile that reached his eyes. Then, with his free hand, he clapped Vale's shoulder. "As it should be. You can't know how happy this makes me." Then he looked down at me. "I would very much like to remain friends, though."

Vale had already said as much, so I knew this was for me to decide. "I would like that too, Sidric. Your friendship means a lot to me."

"Me too, Lyra." He bowed his head before looking back at Vale. "You're much bigger in person. I've watched you play. You're a beast."

Vale barked out a laugh, and just like that, my former lover and my mate were buddies. As it should be, like Sidric had said.

The rest of his team surrounded us after that, and I dutifully met each and every one of them. They were all welcoming and eager to meet me, not to mention excited for their teammate. With each introduction, I felt more at ease with our bond.

More than one of them said some variation of, "Now, he can focus on the game and stop talking about his future mate."

In a short time, I discovered that Vale was a romantic, and his amorous declaration when we'd first met was more than pretty words. He'd truly meant it and had been waiting his whole life to express his feelings to me. My heart swelled with the realization, and I enthusiastically engaged with his peers, pressing myself against his side as he held me close.

The pain and loss I'd felt after Axel's rejection were suddenly so far removed I could barely feel them. I was so overjoyed with hope and acceptance that I wanted to burst into tears.

"There's someone else I want to introduce you to. I'd never miss the championship, but I'm also here to support my buddy. We grew up together. My family is Summer Court, obviously. Go Hornets." Vale winked at me. "My best friend is Spring Court, though, so it was easy for us since we live nearby. Our parents met and became friends through their work as Noble Council members of the realms."

He wasn't bragging or posturing, just informing me. I appreciated the candor and lack of self-importance in his admission. He was a noble son, but it wasn't his personality or identity. He'd said it offhandedly like it wasn't something that should factor into our relationship. He was right—it shouldn't.

We meandered toward a section of the party that was overrun with Starball players. They were mostly from our team, but several were from the other academies.

Vale greeted a large group of students, bumping fists and tapping forearms in typical bro-dude style. It was cute.

"Where's Ace?" he asked one of his teammates.

The male shrugged as he drained his beer and wiped his mouth. "Fuck if I know. I thought he went to get us beers, but he hasn't come back yet."

Vale looked around, and we kept moving. He pointed out players on his team, telling me their names and positions. I wasn't retaining much of the information since I was more focused on the way his lips moved, and how genuinely friendly and well-liked he was.

"Ah, there he is." He stuck his fingers in his mouth and whistled. "Hey!" he called, then his brow furrowed and his tone shifted into confusion. "Dude, what the fuck?"

I turned to look, and that's when the pieces fell into place.

Axel stared at us as he stumbled backward, his steps unsteady.

I tensed, and Vale looked down at me questioningly, but my eyes were focused on Axel. He tried to retreat, but he kept bumping into people behind him.

"Where did you go? You were right beside me when the most amazing thing in my life happened," Vale asked him casually. He was either unaware of the tension between Axel and me or trying hard to ignore it.

"Yeah..." Axel's voice was tight as he flicked his eyes to me and then back to Vale. "I have to go—"

"Shit, you two probably know each other! Don't you?" Vale's smile grew. "Axel, meet my mate, Lyra." He tightened his hold around me and kissed the top of my head. "Isn't she beautiful?"

Chapter Two

The silence was awkward and long enough to be noticeable.

I stared at Axel, and he stared at me. Then he opened his mouth and broke my heart even more. "Yes, she is. So very beautiful." His voice was reverent, and my breath caught. He must have realized what he'd said too late because his features shuttered, and he looked lost for a split second. He shook himself and glanced at Vale. "I ... I'm sorry. I have to go ... somewhere else." He flicked his eyes to me, then back to his friend. "Congratulations, V. You deserve her. You deserve all the happiness in the realms."

With that, Axel spun around and shoved his way through the crowd, moving as far away from us as possible.

"What the fuck, man?" Vale yelled after him, but he didn't leave my side. "What was that about?" Vale asked no one in particular.

"Typical," Puck grumbled as he came to a halt by my side.

"What did he do now?" Roko asked, standing next to my brother. I hadn't realized they had all followed, but I was relieved to have them there.

"He better not have done anything," Puck snapped. "He was told to stay away."

Callie stood in front of me and proceeded to check me over like she was looking for evidence of an attack. "Are you alright? Did he say anything to you, Lyra?"

"No." I shook my head and tried to give them my best "shut the fuck up" look, but it was too late.

"What do you mean?" Vale asked. "Why are you saying these things about my best friend to my mate?"

Everyone froze, and their eyes bounced between me and Vale.

"Awkward," Brev whispered from the other side of Vale.

"That asshole is your BFF?" Sidric sneered.

"Oof, points lost, man." Jed shook his head and threw his arm around Callie. "I get that we just met, but that's not going to go over well with our pr—" His voice cut off with a cough as the geas shut him up. "Pal, Lyra," he wheezed.

Vale glanced at the group and carefully turned to look at me like he was scared he would spook me if he moved too fast.

"I need to know what they're talking about, and I'd prefer if you told me now, my mate." His voice was stern but gentle. He wasn't trying to be demanding, but he was desperate for information.

I understood. We were talking about his best friend, after all.

"Um." I bit my lip and looked around for help, only to find my friends nodding at me with encouragement. "Maybe we don't have to talk about this right now? We just found each other."

"Which is why it's important for me to understand. You are my mate, and there is clearly some negative history between you and Axel. He's like my family—my *brother*." He lifted his hand and swept it down the side of my face. "I need to know why there is discord between you, so I can deal with it. Tell me everything. It's critical I have all the facts and details to make the right choice."

I sucked in a breath and stepped back. Was he telling me he'd choose Axel? Would Vale pick him over me?

Was I about to be rejected again?

His brow wrinkled at the space I'd put between us, and his hand stilled in the air. Then his jaw locked as he ground his teeth together.

My friends moved closer.

"I see." His voice dropped low. His chest swelled as he pulled in a long, calming breath before turning his dark gaze to Sidric. "Tell me. *Now.*" The tone he used with Sidric wasn't the gentle one he had used with me, and the air around us grew hotter as it crackled with his power.

Sidric's face hardened in response. "I will warn you that if you react negatively, you will not like the result."

He jerked his head, and we followed as he led us toward an empty fire pit away from the dense crowd.

Vale kept pace with Sidric as we walked, and Puck was on his heels, so Roko took my side. Callie took the other as we trailed behind them with Jed and Brev.

"Explain," Vale demanded when Sidric stopped and turned to face him again.

He couldn't tell him the whole truth. None of us could—not yet, anyway. Not until he passed his mate-magic tasks.

Sidric glared at Vale. "First, you should understand that, around here, your buddy's a fucking prick and no friend of ours."

He went on to give Vale a detailed explanation of how Axel had treated me since I arrived at Araphel Academy and how his girlfriend and her friends had taken up ranks. Callie added her two cents when she thought Sidric wasn't giving a complete story, and the others tossed out a few things Axel had said during practice and games—only some of which I was aware of.

Puck didn't say much. He flicked his eyes to me every once in a while, keeping his jaw locked tight. I guessed he let everyone else take the lead in the story to keep up appearances.

Vale's face hardened and his hands balled into fists, but he remained still. He didn't look at me or move to my side. He just listened with thinly veiled anger on his face.

It reminded me so much of Axel that I started preparing myself for his rejection.

Sidric got to the honey incident, and Callie, Puck, and Roko wrapped their arms around me. When Callie told him I'd stopped breathing and my heart nearly failed, Vale exploded. Literally.

His fire magic pulsed out of him, and the flames in the pit in front of us shot past the trees and into the sky. He roared, and his fiery gaze turned to me.

I froze.

I knew what his shifted animal was without any doubt as the fire-gold rings of his dragon peered back at me.

His footfalls were heavy as he closed the distance between us. I could feel them reverberating in the ground, and I imagined the mantle cracking under his foot.

I went rigid.

I wasn't entirely sure what was about to happen, but my eyes swam as my heart pounded in my chest.

Vale practically yanked me away from Callie and Puck, and crushed me against him so tightly that the air puffed out of my lungs. He was breathing hard as he held me against him. Then, he bent and scooped me into his arms, nuzzling my neck as he breathed in my scent.

Everyone froze at his reaction. It wasn't just that he was a massive, pissed-off male or that his fire magic was so impressive that it burned the night sky—his dragon was practically breathing fire and growling so low that the dirt on the ground quivered.

He was a fearsome beast, and everyone knew it but no one moved. He wasn't giving off dangerous energy, just possessive determination.

Vale kissed up my neck frantically before looking into my eyes and crushing his lips to mine. He pulled away and hugged me, tucking me safely into his arms. When his breathing slowed and the growling finally stopped, he spun to face Sidric.

"She's obviously fine now. But I know there's more, and I need to hear the rest," Vale said, not making any attempt to let me go. "I have to know everything before I deal with him."

He still wanted me. He wasn't rejecting me, and he was upset with his friend.

I melted into his hold. My exhale was heavy as I secured myself around him and let the tears spill down my cheeks.

Vale tightened his arms around me. "You are safe with me, my mate. No one will ever harm you again," he vowed.

Sidric told Vale the rest of the story. The others joined in again, but their tones were considerably more friendly. They'd all been prepared to watch another of my mates reject me—I was sure of that now. Even though it was virtually unheard of, Axel had fractured the belief that mate bonds were unequivocally sacred and wanted. They were leery of what they had never thought to question before, and it was sad how far Axel's betrayal had reached.

Vale stared at me when they finished. "You've been through too much already, and at the hands of someone I called brother, no less. I'm not comfortable being away from you after hearing this. I am in full control of my dragon, but you must know I am riding a fine line right now. I want to kill the one who hurt you, and that desire is at war with my need to protect you, claim you, and hide you away like the treasure you are. I know we just met, and we have a lot to learn about each other, but I will put in a transfer first thing tomorrow. Even if it takes weeks, I will not leave your side. I'll pull strings, and use my family name and connections if I have to. I thought you would come to High Crest with me, but you need your friends. They have protected you and supported you. I won't ask you to leave them for me."

"You would come here? For me?"

He reared back. "Of course. I would do anything for you. You are my mate, Lyra. Why would you question that?"

I shook my head. "I don't know how this works," I told him truthfully.

My experience with mates had shattered all my preconceived notions and expectations. Watching my parents and brothers over the years had given me false hope. I wasn't sure what to believe after Axel, so everything with Vale would be new.

His eyes softened. "I have never had a mate, but I promise you, this is how it works." He kissed me again and set me on my feet. "I need a drink. Would you like one?"

I nodded. "I would."

"Good thing there's a keg we can steal for ourselves." Brev jerked his thumb over his shoulder, and without another word, Vale followed him. They each took a side and carried the keg closer to the group.

Some people protested, but they followed to get a refill of their beers and left after they had their drinks. When my cup was full, I found a log to sit on and took a sip. The happy buzz I'd had before meeting Vale was gone, and I wasn't interested in getting it back, either.

Vale sat next to me and gulped half his beer, licking the foam from his top lip as he finished. He grabbed my hand and lifted it to his mouth to kiss my fingers. "We have a lot to talk about."

"We do." I smiled at him. "But I have to ask, are you sure you want to come here? What about Starball?"

He shook his head. "I'm sure. Besides, I'll play here. Half of your team is graduating this year. There'll be plenty of room for me."

"I feel bad..."

"Don't. This was always a possibility. The only reason I wasn't already attending Araphel was to keep an eye on my sister. She met both of her mates last summer, and that changed our plans. We were going to come here, but they both attended High Crest, and she didn't want to make them readjust for her since they were already established there. She's busy with her bond group and doesn't need me breathing down her neck, anyway. I was always meant to be here, and now I will be—with you."

Noble families usually sent their children to Araphel Academy, so what he'd said made sense.

"Okay," I said, blushing under his watchful eye.

"I'll get my own dorm room. I don't want to pressure you into anything you're not ready for. But maybe we'll be in a mated room by next year?"

My cheeks warmed. I wasn't sure why I felt so shy about the possibility of intimacy. I'd never been timid before, and he was my mate. But maybe that was precisely the reason. Before, I'd known it was just a temporary entanglement—it hadn't really mattered. This *did* matter, and it certainly wasn't temporary. I'd be with this male for the rest of our lives. Suddenly, I felt insecure about whether I'd measure up to his previous partners.

As if he could read my mind, Vale put his cup down and pulled me onto his lap. He put a finger under my chin and tipped my face toward him. "You're perfect, and whatever put this frown on your face doesn't matter. We just met, Lyra, but I promise I will never want anyone as much as I want you."

I lifted my hand to brush his hair from his forehead. "I don't know why I'm nervous. I feel silly."

"You're not." He kissed the tip of my nose. "We'll learn how to do this together, but for now, know there is nothing you could ever say or do that would make me not want this bond with you. You're mine, Lyra, and I intend to have you forever."

Chapter Three

"I'll come by in the morning, and we can get breakfast before the game," Vale said, standing outside my dorm. It was more of a statement than a question, but I eagerly agreed.

My bond thrummed in my chest. His need to be close made me feel desired and wanted, and I liked that very much. "I can't wait."

His broad smile made my heart flutter, and my own countenance mirrored his joy.

"Good." He bent down and kissed me. "I'll see you tomorrow," he whispered against my mouth.

I bit my lip and kept my eyes on his as I closed the door. He didn't move until the lock engaged, and then I heard his heavy footfalls echo down the hallway.

I squealed silently, and threw myself on my bed and chirped into my pillow, kicking my feet like a teen with a crush. I supposed it wasn't that far off. It was better, though, because my crush was my mate, and I knew that this feeling would never fade.

Rolling over, I stared at the ceiling in disbelief. I knew I'd find more of my mates one day, but it was surreal after everything I'd gone through with Axel. I struggled to wrap my mind around it. I wanted to scream from the rooftop that I'd found my mate—and he wanted me as much as I wanted him.

I settled for a shower.

A little over an hour later, I was getting ready to crawl into bed when someone knocked on my door.

I jumped at the sound and tentatively walked to the entry. "Who is it?"

"It's me," a deep voice replied.

I opened the wooden barrier and found a distraught-looking Vale leaning against the frame. When his eyes met mine, they were filled with pain. Ushering him inside, I flipped the lock and led him straight to my couch to check him over.

His fists were busted up and bleeding, his hair was mussed, his clothes were dirty, and his head was heavy as he rested it in his palms.

"Goddess, are you alright?" I asked. I wasn't a healer, but we could heal ourselves and our mates to some extent.

My instincts flared to life, needing to take away his pain. Without thinking or asking, I restored his hands to the perfect condition they were in when he'd left me a short while ago.

He glanced down at his newly mended knuckles and sighed. "No. I'm not okay. I'm angry. I'm fucking angry and hurt." He looked up and pulled me onto his lap until I was straddling his thighs. "I'm devastated and so sorry, Lyra. You didn't tell me..." He shuddered and closed his eyes, hugging me tight.

His arms were like steel bars wrapped around me, and I held him to me just as desperately. I'd been unprepared for his sudden arrival and clueless about what happened to him since he'd left, but I needed him as much as he seemed to need me right now.

"What's the matter? Please tell me what happened. Why are you so upset?"

He shook his head and burrowed his face into my shoulder. It took him a few minutes to speak, and when he finally did, his breathing was shallow. "He rejected you."

His words were so quiet I barely heard them, but they poured over me like ice water.

I froze.

He held me tighter, which reassured me enough to admit the truth. I nodded my confirmation, and he shivered.

Confessing this to Vale unleashed the emotions I'd buried, and the sting of what Axel had done felt raw as it ripped through me all over again. It was a visceral pain, and in the arms of a mate that wanted me, I was as tender and bruised as I'd been the night it happened. Because it wasn't only my pain anymore, it was Vale's, too, and not because he was my mate. Axel's rejection had affected the entire bond group. He'd rejected him—no, he'd rejected *us*. Just like he'd rejected the others that would follow. Axel's betrayal would always be heart-wrenching, but it was worse for Vale because they were so close. Some people dreamed of being in the same bond as their friends. By Vale's reaction, I guessed he was one of them. He was a romantic, and how great would it have been to share your love with your best friend?

Mate groups came in all forms. Some were fully mated, with every member romantically involved with one another. Others had a core bond, where everyone revolved around a central figure. And then there were variations that blended the two.

Bond-mates could be siblings, cousins, friends, or they could have a romantic connection. In all groups, the relationships between bond-mates were as important as the connection to the mated individual, regardless of their romantic involvement.

Our bonds transcended traditional relationships, binding us together in ways that surpassed ordinary connections. We felt each other, shared our power and strength. We were whole and complete when together, and finding our bonds filled empty spaces in our very being that we didn't know existed until they were no longer void.

"I'm so sorry, Lyra," he murmured a while later. "I know why you didn't tell me. I understand, and I'm not upset with you."

I hadn't thought he was upset with me, but it was still nice to hear.

"I heard the rumors about what happened at Spring Equinox, but I didn't believe them. I would never have thought he was capable of something like that. I was so sure of him as a person that I didn't have to ask. I didn't want to disrespect him by bringing up such a heinous lie." He shook his head. "I've always believed him. I trusted him about everything since we became friends, and in a lot of ways, I put him above everyone else. He was my best friend, my brother, and..." He let out a breath. "I'm not justifying his actions. I'm explaining, not giving him an excuse. I just want you to know."

I encouraged him to continue.

"His family hasn't always been prominent in court. But his father..." He ground his teeth and looked away. "His father is a power-hungry leech. He's been gaining power in court for years. He's awful to his wife and their children, always putting his ambitions above anything else. Axel hated him, hated how he acted. The things his dad said and did in the name of power." He tipped his head back and blew out a frustrated breath. "I don't understand how it came to this, how I didn't see that Axel wasn't being corrupted by his dad but instead becoming like him. He told me why he rejected you."

He closed his eyes and took several deep breaths. His body went rigid under me as he attempted to calm himself.

"He told me what he said and did. He rejected you, believing he would be granted another chance—another mate. One with supposedly more power and connections. It's disgusting," he spat. "I lost it. I'm not a violent person, Lyra. Not normally." He looked up at me with big, pleading eyes. "I don't use my size and power against anyone, especially those who can't match me. But I lost it tonight, and I hope you can forgive me because I beat him. I beat him until he was unrecognizable. I had to be pulled off of him by your friends. If they hadn't," he said, shuddering, "I don't know what would have happened."

He sat up straight and held my face in his hands. "Lyra, you are my mate. We've barely talked about anything, but I want you to know—I *need* you to know—that none of that matters to me. I don't care if you aren't from a noble house. I don't mind if you possess only modest magic abilities. I want you. I wanted you before we ever met. You're perfect exactly as you are, and I will always choose you. I chose you the moment I laid eyes on you, but I need you to hear me. I've put him first time and time again, and I shouldn't have. I've put my loyalty to him above all others, including my family at times, but that is no more. I cannot accept someone in my life or allow someone around you that believes what he does. Axel has been my best friend and brother since we were small children, but now he is not. I've rejected him. He is not my friend. He is not my brother. He is not my bond-mate. He is a stranger to me. You are everything, Lyra, and I will protect you with my life. I will protect you from him or anyone else that would threaten you."

As he spoke each word with sincerity and conviction, I could feel the weight of the geas gradually lifting, its grip on me weakening with each passing moment. Emotions welled up within me, and tears streamed down my face, uncontrollably mirroring the depth of my overwhelming relief and joy. He had proven himself worthy, not through displays of magical prowess but through the embodiment of qualities that truly mattered.

The link that bound us together offered a glimpse into the tests he had passed, though Vale alone truly comprehended their depth. While I couldn't fully discern the intricate details, I could feel it in the way he looked at me and in the unwavering dedication he had displayed since we first met.

The first test he'd passed was acceptance of the mate bond—a bond forged by fate and intertwined destinies. Without hesitation, he'd embraced it, recognizing the profound connection we shared and the responsibility that came with it.

Though, for me, it was his unwavering loyalty that spoke volumes and stood as a testament to the depth of his commitment. This act of choosing and proving his loyalty stood as the pinnacle of importance and filled me with a sense of security, knowing that he had chosen me unconditionally, forsaking all others.

Within myself and my own magic, it was that very moment—when I embraced his acceptance and wholeheartedly trusted in his proven commitment—that the geas was triggered and began to dissolve.

His features shifted when magic swelled around us, and the room seemed to glow as it slipped away.

"Please understand..." I whispered as I stood from his lap.

He froze in place, confusion clear on his features as he tried to discern what was happening. There would be nothing in comparison to draw on. He could only sit back and watch.

Seeing the geas slip away and reveal my true form could be shocking, and I'd been taught to give my bonds space when it happened.

It was also different because, unlike when I'd been attacked, this was intentional. That had been accidental, and as my life and magic slipped away, there'd been no fanfare—just a desperate plea from my magic for someone to save me.

He covered his mouth as he watched the enchantment manifest and swirl around me. I had been wearing pajamas moments ago, but now, I stood before him in a regal gown with a crown on my head. My dress was black and studded with diamonds, like the night sky. My hair fell around my shoulders, and atop my head was a crown that held the Night Kingdom's onyx jewel. I looked ready for a ball.

"Goddess... You're..." He didn't finish whatever he was trying to say. He just stared.

"I'm sorry it had to be this way." My voice was quieter than I wanted it to be. I knew he wouldn't reject me, but I still felt unsure and shy. "I would never lie to you or deceive you willingly. This is a vow I make to you now. I never will again. It's a rule..."

"I know, my love." He moved to stand in front of me. "We all know about the secrecy of the bond between the Queen and her Knights. Not the specifics, but we know she's hidden until they prove themselves worthy. I'm not upset with you. I'm shocked to my core. I don't feel betrayed or deceived. I'm in awe. I don't feel worthy of you. You're ... the Night Princess."

Chapter Four

"And you're my Summer Knight."

Vale's whole body shivered. His head bowed, then he dropped to one knee before me. "You are my Night Princess and, one day, will be my Queen. I pledge myself to you—my loyalty, my fealty, and my love. I don't know if I'm worthy, but I will endeavor to spend my life trying. Lyra, my fated mate, I accepted you the moment I knew you. Do you accept me and our bond?"

This male was a hopeless romantic, and I was utterly besotted.

I used my magic to evanesce the dress and crown back into the ether, where it would wait for me to reveal myself again. Clad in pajamas once more, I dropped to my knees in front of him, grabbed his hands, and held them to my chest. "I accept you, and I accept our bond. Forever and always. Never bow to me again. You will stand by my side, never lower or higher. You are my mate, and we are equal in all things."

He stood, pulling me with him. Our lips crashed together in a passionate kiss. There was so much we needed to discuss, so many things we had yet to learn about each other, but this was us. This was what it meant to have a fated-mate connection that transcended everything. We were one. We were made for each other, and we were going to cement our bond here and now. The rest would come later.

I pulled my shirt over my head. I wore nothing beneath my sleep clothes, and if his look of surprise was anything to go by, he hadn't expected things to go this far. He tightened his hold on me, groaning low and deep.

"Fuck, are you sure?" He peppered my lips with kisses. "I want you so badly, but we have time if you're not ready."

"I'm sure. I want you. I want this. I want to complete our bond."

I trusted our magic, and most of all, I trusted him. I knew he was mine. It rang true in my soul, and I didn't want to wait. I didn't need to.

"You're mine, Summer Knight. Make me yours."

He moaned a deep, sexy groan that I was already addicted to. It vibrated between my thighs, making me ache. My dorm was modest in size, so he only had to take a few steps to get to my bedroom.

As he walked, I worked the hem of his shirt up, and when he sat me on the bed, he finished ripping it off. Kneeling, I pressed my face into his skin and ran my hands up his muscled chest. He was toned, but his skin was soft and warm. I kissed his stomach and his pecs, and when I pulled one of his nipples between my lips and flicked it with my tongue, he pushed his fingers into my hair. He fisted the locks, tipped my head back, and leaned in for a searing kiss. Splitting my lips apart with his own, he tangled his tongue with mine.

I undid his pants, and shimmied them over his hips and down his thighs, where they stayed as I greedily fisted his cock. He jerked in my hand and grunted as I stroked his length, circling the head, and pushed down to the base repeatedly.

"Fuck, Princess, you're gonna make me come, and I haven't even tasted you yet."

He laid me flat on the bed and kissed down my body, removing my shorts and panties along the way. When I was bare, he took himself in his hand and pumped as he devoured me with his eyes.

"You're fucking gorgeous." He licked his lips as he shoved his pants the rest of the way off.

Vale climbed on the bed, put his hands on my thighs, and spread me open.

"Look at that pretty little pussy, all wet and aching for me." He slipped a finger through my silky arousal, and the contact had my nipples tightening.

The leaky head of his cock told me he was as eager as I was. Our desire for each other was evident, but our need to bond also pushed us together. He dropped between my thighs, and without any preamble, he closed his lips around my clit and sucked me into his mouth.

I cried out from the intensity, my back bowing off the bed as my hands fisted the sheets beneath us. He spread me further, keeping me in place as he kissed me intimately with his entire mouth.

I was a panting, writhing mess for him in a short time, and when I begged him for more, he hummed into my needy sex.

"Please, please," I whined as I rolled my hips.

He twirled my clit with his tongue, using enough pressure to work me up but not get me off. His hand moved from my thigh, and suddenly, his thick fingers pushed into my core, feeling incredible as they slid in and out, stretching me as I clenched around him, desperate for more friction.

"That's it. Squeeze my fingers. Show me what you're going to do to me with this tight little pussy," he mumbled around my wet flesh as he pumped his fingers into me. "Come for me, beautiful. Give me your sweetness," Vale ordered.

He curled his fingers as he sucked my clit in a pulsing tempo that had me orgasming in his mouth, just as he'd told me to. My toes curled, my back bowed, my nipples pebbled, and a long, low moan tore from my throat.

Vale kept up his ministrations, only relenting when I went limp beneath him. He kissed up my body, leaving a wet trail as he moved over my skin. When he reached my breasts, he gave each one a lick before finally taking my mouth again.

Wrapping my legs around his waist, I pulled his face down to mine as he settled between my thighs. Reaching down, I moved his straining erection up and down my sopping center, getting his thick cock wet. Then I angled him down, and his fat mushroom head slipped inside.

He groaned, dropping his head to suck on my breasts before he sat up on his knees, pushing open my legs and zeroing in on where we were barely joined.

"I'm going to fuck this pussy and make it mine," he growled, rocking his hips.

"Yes," I gasped and lifted my hips to push myself on him.

He wrapped his hands around my waist and squeezed. "Mine," he declared, thrusting while pulling me down until my hips were flush with his.

It felt so fucking good.

He was huge—bigger than any other male I'd ever been with—and the stretch was the perfect balance of pleasure and pain. I felt him like a second skin, and it was amazing.

We moved in perfect harmony. He lifted my body up and down his length as he worked himself into me, and when he bottomed out, he ground against me, pleasuring my clit against his hot flesh.

He circled his hips again and again until I was clawing at the bed. He was in charge, but I clenched and pulled him into me, taking and giving equally. The room was hot, and we were both lost in the pleasure of our merging.

When we came together, everything snapped into place in an overwhelmingly powerful orgasm. My whole body felt the release, and it lasted longer than I'd thought possible. Vale spilled deep inside me, and we stared at each other as our magic mingled, intertwining our essences and binding our souls.

I could sense his joy, the same way he could sense mine.

After what felt like a small eternity of bliss, he covered me with his body and kissed me until the pleasure waned and the bond settled into place. He held me as our bodies thrummed with aftershocks.

"My Princess," he crooned as his hands traced my curves, exploring every inch of my skin with reverence as warmth coursed through our connection.

"My mate," I whispered, closing my eyes and surrendering to the deeper bond.

We were lost in our own world, oblivious to everything around us, as two halves of a whole united in a spiritual nexus that transcended the physical realm.

Chapter Five

We showered together, slowly exploring each other as we rinsed off. Falling asleep in Vale's arms had been as natural as breathing, and waking up with him was a dream come true.

"Good morning." His gravelly voice was low next to my ear, and he pressed his hardening dick into my ass cheeks.

I arched against him. "Good morning."

"If we have time before your friends get here, I'm more than happy to fill you up again, my mate." He kissed my neck, wrapped his hands around me, and held me tight.

Looking at the clock, I was disappointed. "You shouldn't have said anything. Now I *know* we don't have time."

He chuckled as he rolled me over, his sleepy face even more handsome because it was special and just for me. "We'll go to the game and spend time with your friends, but afterward, I want to take you to dinner and discuss how we move forward. Is that alright?"

I smiled at him. "I'll go anywhere with you, but yes, we can discuss anything you'd like throughout the day. We don't have to wait."

"I thought the geas would prevent me from speaking of such things?"

"It does. Mostly. We can talk about many other things that have nothing to do with our positions." His eyes widened. "It's not only my geas now; it's yours too. You're a Knight, Vale."

He was quiet for a moment. "Holy shit."

"Are you okay? This is a lot."

He leaned in to kiss me. "It is, but I'm happy for it all. I'm still blown away and so fucking excited that I have a mate. I'm in awe that she's my Princess. Never in my wildest dreams did I consider ever being a Knight, but to hear you say it ... it makes it real."

"You didn't ask for this..."

"I want you, Lyra. I asked the goddess for you, my mate, and I'll accept everything that comes with the bond. If you were a troll and I had to collect the toll at your bridge, I'd be just as thrilled with that, too." I giggled as he stamped kisses along my neck. "You said we can discuss most things, but what does that mean?" he asked, settling back against the pillow.

I put my hand on his cheek. "We can speak freely with my family and Puck's mate, Roko. Also, my friends know everything."

"What? How?"

"When I was ... struggling after the honey incident."

He went rigid, and his lips curved into a scowl. "Dying. You mean when you were attacked and nearly murdered."

"Shh." I brushed a finger over his mouth. "If you were hurt, I would be just as upset, but don't be angry on my account. I haven't forgotten, but I've moved on. He made his choice, and what happened was a result of that. I don't believe they'll ever harm me again, so I've decided to move forward and not dwell on the past. And now I have you."

"Yes, you do." He kissed me. "And nothing like that will ever happen again. I gave you my word, and I meant it. You're mine to love, protect, and honor. I take that very seriously."

"I know. I can feel it." I rubbed my chest where I sensed the link between us. "Let's not talk about that right now, though. I only wanted you to know that when my glamour failed that day, Callie, Sidric, Jed, Brev, and Professor Warrock were there when it happened. They immediately recognized my true identity, like you did when the geas lifted, but they acted fast and kept me hidden until my family could take me home. They were brought in and placed under the geas order too."

"They know everything?"

"Yes, including the truth of the Spring Equinox. So, while none of us can say anything to reveal my identity, we can speak freely with each other. It makes it so much easier when I can be honest." I giggled. "If I hadn't almost died, I would thank Jana for giving me such a gift."

Vale didn't laugh, but I could see in his eyes that he understood. "We'll discuss everything while getting to know each other throughout the day."

"And we'll probably have to see my parents after the game. Which is another reason why we shouldn't save getting to know each other more for later. They'll have questions," I told him as I ran my fingers through his hair.

"You want me to meet the Queen and her Knights?" He sat up and looked at me like I'd told him I was from the moon.

"My mother and my fathers," I corrected. "Yes. You are my mate, and you will meet my parents."

"But ... so soon?"

I snorted and climbed on his lap because he was mine and I could. He wrapped his arms around my waist and settled me where he wanted before running his hands over my bare skin. It was all so natural.

"Is my big, strong dragon scared to meet my parents?" I teased.

He smirked and tugged me closer. "Am I still wrapping my head around the fact that, less than a day ago, I met my mate, discovered she is the Night Princess, and had her elevate my status from noble son to Knight? Or that she wants to take me home to meet the Queen and her fathers, the Knight Lords? Who also happen to be our protectors, balance keepers, and the strongest fae among us because of their connection to magic and the mate-bond they share. No. I'm totally fine. Everyday stuff for me, love."

I chuckled. "If you need more time, they will understand. There is absolutely no pressure."

"Hell no. I might be intimidated and unsure of what I'm doing, but I'm by your side. My life is with you, and I'm ready to live it."

"Good." I kissed him and put up a privacy spell around the room. Then I lifted onto my knees, angled myself over his hardness, and slid myself down onto him.

"Oh, fuck." He grunted and looked down at where we were joined in surprise. "I thought..." He moaned when I rolled over him. "We didn't..." He groaned long and low as I circled my waist, grinding myself onto him as I rolled my hips. "...have time," he panted but then stopped talking and went to work.

He guided my movements like the night before, but this time I was on top. I pushed my fingers into his hair and fisted the locks as we sped up our movements, using it for leverage as he moved my body over him to his will.

"Yes," he growled. "Come for me. Come on my cock, Princess. Make me wet with your sweetness."

He moved his hand to thumb over my clit, and I did as he'd asked. I clenched and spasmed around him, and he groaned when his orgasm followed mine a few pumps later. We collapsed on the bed, breathing hard, and every time I twitched around his softening sex, he jerked inside of me.

We showered together, and he dressed in his clothes from yesterday since that was all he had to wear. Our first stop would be to his temporary dorm so he could change before the game, and when I opened the door to leave, I found Callie with her hand up as if she was going to knock on my forehead.

She squealed. "Holy shit, I almost whacked your head!"

I laughed and watched her eyes grow big when she saw Vale behind me. He was a huge male, but I didn't think that was why she was shocked to see him.

"Uh ... hello, Lyra's mate."

"Hello, Lyra's best friend."

She smirked at me as he closed the door behind us. "What the hell happened to your clothes?" she asked when she caught sight of his scuffed outfit.

He tugged me into his arms. "I confronted my ex-best friend last night about what you told me. He confirmed what you all know to be true, and I kicked his ass. Actually, your other friends had to pull me off of him. They'll have the details. Then I came here and..." He glanced down at me in question.

I looked at Callie. "And he knows."

Her eyes widened. "Like, he knows..."

"Everything. The same as you. I've already sent word to my parents, and we have to see them after the game."

"Oh snap! So, this is... You're..." She looked up at him. "You'll be ... you know, someday. Damn, do I have to bow to you now or some shit too?"

"You're silly. Nothing changes, remember?" I laughed and told Vale. "They're still wrapping their heads around everything."

I shared with him stories of my friends and their struggles to adjust as we walked to his room.

"Thank fuck I'm not alone. My brain sort of exploded last night," he said, miming the top of his head blowing off.

"I know what you mean." Callie nodded as we exited the building. "Lyra's the sweetest, chillest Pri— ... chick I've ever met, and it's not what I expected. Not that I ever met a person like her or expected to be friends with the future Q— ... you know? It's normal for her, I get it, and we're all doing our best to be normal too."

"But it's a mindfuck."

"Total mindfuck," Callie agreed. "Never in my life would I have thought I'd be close to this ... and now she's my best friend."

"You're all doing great," I assured them as they shared in their mutual existential crisis. "I can appreciate that it's a lot for you all. But really, you're all amazing."

Vale squeezed me, and he bent to kiss the top of my head. "You're amazing."

We reached the temporary dorms, and as Vale changed, I told him we'd come by later to get his things so he could spend the night again. We had a few days off after the game, and my parents might ask us to stay at the castle.

We fell in line with the crowd as we made our way to the stadium. Vale joined me in the Araphel student section, even though he'd originally planned to sit with his team. He was determined not to leave my side and wouldn't even consider sitting with his friends when I suggested it.

"Not gonna happen, mate. You're stuck with me." He smirked as we weaved through the horde of students.

When we reached our seats, I turned in his arms and stood on my tiptoes. He ducked down so I could whisper in his ear, "I like being stuck with you."

His smile was as bright as the sun, and when he stood to his full height, he lifted me with him and kissed me in front of the entire student section. His PDA earned a rousing round of applause, including whoops from the guys and squeals from the gals. Then they all chanted, "Mate, mate, mate."

Their enthusiasm only encouraged him. He held me up with one arm and pumped his other fist in the air while they shouted. I was a little embarrassed at all the attention, but I was proud to be his, so I smiled and went along with it.

Making out in front of an audience wasn't generally celebrated, but since we'd found each other in front of half the student body, they were eager to celebrate our mating.

It was very exciting.

Vale put me down, and we all focused on the field when music boomed through the stadium.

The announcers introduced the Day Court team, and their side roared as the players ran onto the field. The cheerleaders formed a tunnel, and their mascots cartwheeled along the sideline, using magic and confetti to hype up the attendees.

When our team was introduced, everyone went wild. The stadium erupted with fireworks and magical displays, and the music was so loud I could feel it in my bones. Our team went through a shadow tunnel crafted by my mother that was marbled and accented with each of my father's elements. The effect was badass, and the crowd went crazy. The volume increased as the team emerged onto the field, where our cheerleaders and mascots were doing their own routine.

As the defending champs, our team received extra time and a special introduction since we had the home-field advantage.

When the captains were introduced, Vale turned to me with wide eyes. "Fucking hell. Puck is... How did I not think of that until right now?"

I laughed, waving to Puck and Roko. I didn't know if they saw us, but they fist-pumped the air when they looked at the student section.

The players were next, and we hollered our support for Brev, Jed, Sidric, and the rest of the Silver and Black Squads.

When Axel's name echoed through the stadium, he zeroed in on Vale and me like he knew exactly where we were in the sea of students. He must have had a healer attend to him because he wasn't as beat up as I'd expected, but he still looked worse for wear. His eyes darted back and forth, alternating between Vale and me.

Vale wrapped his arm around me, pulling me closer and positioning me slightly behind him. It was as if he sought to shield me from Axel's gaze, using his own body as a protective barrier.

Axel's eyes traced the path of Vale's arm as it enveloped me, and a flicker of annoyance pinched his expression with Vale's attempt to conceal me from him.

When his gaze shifted back to Vale, a prolonged stare ensued between the two, and the already tangible tension—which had been building between them across the field—grew even more palpable.

As the opening ceremonies drew to a close, Axel's attention shifted toward me, and I swore I could feel his gaze sweeping over every inch of my face before locking onto my eyes. We held each other's gaze long enough for it to be noticeable, and Vale tightened his hold around me ever so slightly.

Axel's shoulders dropped, and when he turned away to join the rest of the team, his head bowed.

When Axel was out of sight, Vale relaxed his hold on me. I put my hand on his chest and looked up at him. "I don't begrudge you for what you did to him last night. It's why you came to me after, and because of that, our bond is complete." He gazed down at me with a wrinkle between his brows. "But I hope the ass beating you gave him doesn't affect the game." I smirked, and all the tension left his body when he realized I was teasing him.

"You should know your mate here is a super fan," Callie chimed in beside me. "Bravo on working his face over but, dude, you couldn't wait until after the game?"

Vale blurted out a laugh. "You're lucky he's walking. Or breathing." He winked at me, but I knew he was serious. We both had strong feelings on the matter, but as I'd told him earlier, we needed to move forward.

Chapter Six

"Tonight, we celebrate!" Puck yelled to the crowd at the after-party.

Because we'd won the game, my parents had sent word that I could bring Vale home to meet them the following morning. So we joined everyone else, drinks in hand, listening as Puck and Roko made speeches.

The game had been tough, but they'd managed a win, and I was so proud of Puck. He'd led the team to a perfect season, and the championship was the ultimate prize. It was a moment of triumph for the team and validation for him—a testament to his dedication and hard work. He deserved to be recognized at the academy, surrounded by his team, friends, and peers at a postseason championship party.

My parents might be responsible adults and rulers of the kingdom now, but they'd been young once, and they understood the importance of tonight. They'd never take that away from any of us. Meeting my Summer Knight and solidifying our bond was one of those things that timing couldn't have predicted.

We raised our glasses and whooped, cheering their accomplishment.

Vale didn't leave my side once. He had his arm draped over my shoulders if he wasn't holding my hand or touching the small of my back. We leaned into each other, always in contact, but it never felt forced or for show. It was right in every way, and I adored it.

He introduced me to a few of his friends, who'd only arrived in time for the game. He broke the news to them that he'd be transferring to Araphel Academy, and they were surprised we were moving so quickly. Many bonds stayed at their school until the new year, then decided who would transfer where. But that's not what Vale wanted to do. He'd already expressed his reluctance to leave me, even for the few days it would take to arrange the transfer.

They all understood and were happy for us, but they were bummed they'd be losing one of their best players. That opened the door for all kinds of teasing. Through their conversations, I learned that Vale wasn't just a great Starball player—he was a great friend. They all had a story to share. He was funny, caring, and loyal, and though I'd known that from our short time together, it was something else to have it confirmed.

"I remember the first time I met him. I started the season late, and it was my first day on the Starball team. I'd seen him play and was intimidated by his size," Paxon, one of Vale's friends, said.

"And my mad skills, bro." Vale playfully punched him in the shoulder.

"Of course." Paxon rolled his eyes, and they snorted. "I quickly realized that he wasn't just a dominant player but also a prankster."

The others on Vale's team agreed, laughing.

"I was getting ready for my first match, and I was nervous. I'd played Starball my whole life, but never in front of a crowd. We were in the locker room, and suddenly, he turns to me and says, 'You know the best way to beat the other team, right?' I thought he was going to give me some trade secret or something. But he looked me dead in the eye and said, 'Distraction.' Then he walked away. I thought, what kind of stupid advice is that? It wasn't until he was standing at his locker again that I realized the entire room had gone quiet. This motherfucker drops his towel, and out rolls his big old dragon tail! Then he turns to me, gives me a wink, and smacks me on the ass with the flapping thing."

"You liked it," Vale winked at him.

Then, right before our eyes, his tail crept over Paxon's shoulder.

"Asshole." Paxon shoved it off. The group erupted with laughter as he continued, "But the prank didn't stop there. We were walking out onto the court for warm-ups, and I was still baffled that the big, scary dragon shifter had mooned me and spanked me with his tail. So when he points up to the ceiling and yells, 'Look out, it's raining!', I look up like a dummy. That's when I felt cold, wet drops hit my face. I look around, confused, because, duh, we're inside. That's when I see him grinning at me, holding a water bottle and using his air magic to sprinkle it over my head."

Vale grinned. "See, I told you distraction was key."

The group continued to reminisce, assuring me he wasn't all fun and games. He was clearly a dedicated friend, and I loved hearing about him from others. They had no idea what it meant to me.

Hours later, we joined my friends around the fire. The party was going strong. There was loud music and tons of celebration, but instead of getting caught up in all the hoopla, we decided to chill together away from the chaos.

"When are you expected tomorrow?" Puck asked.

I shrugged. "Brunch. She said there's a family dinner planned too."

"Oh, I know. The others have been blowing up my phone all day asking me questions."

I rolled my eyes. They'd been doing the same to me, but I'd told them to be patient and ignored their messages.

"How are you feeling, Vale? You look a little pale," Roko teased.

"You would know."

"Which is why I'm asking." He beamed at him cheekily. "It feels good to be on this side."

"Stop teasing him. You'll make it worse," I whined.

"Make what worse?" Axel slurred, lurching over to our group.

He couldn't have known what we were discussing since it was so vague, but I still didn't like that he'd eavesdropped. He was drunk enough to come over, which made me nervous—especially after what Vale had done to him the night before.

He stumbled into our circle and stood directly in front of Vale and me. He kept his eyes on me as if waiting for me to reply. There was a pleading expression on his face as he scanned my features, his gaze traveling down my body until it finally landed on my and Vale's intertwined hands.

"What are you doing here?" Vale's tone was sharp as he scolded him. "I told you to stay away."

Axel's lips twisted as he flopped onto the log and leaned forward. "V ... please. You ... you're my best friend." He hiccupped, and when he turned to Vale, it became more apparent that he was well and truly drunk. His eyes were bloodshot, and his face was swollen and splotchy.

He wobbled in his seat as he looked at the others, then he cast a privacy spell and returned his attention to Vale. Vale's confusion pulsed through the bond, but before either of us could disband the enchantment, it shattered. Axel was too drunk to hold it, and he didn't notice when it fell.

"I didn't mean to. I didn't know ... she was ... ours," he slurred.

Vale leapt up and jerked Axel to his feet by the collar of his shirt. He yanked him forward and snarled, "What the fuck did you just say?"

Axel's words were a punch to the gut. It felt like he'd knocked the wind out of me, and I grabbed the log to hold myself steady. I wasn't his—not anymore. How dare he say something so cruel and painful.

Axel struggled in Vale's hold, grabbing onto his forearms for balance. "Lyra ... she's—"

"Mine," Vale snapped. "Lyra is mine. My mate. My bond. *Mine.* Not yours." Vale shoved him, and Axel fell to the ground. He grunted at the impact, and his breath left his body in a huff. He didn't move as Vale towered over him. "Don't ever talk about my mate again. She's nothing to you. She never was, and now neither am I. You made your choice, and you fucked up. We're done. I mean it. There's nothing here for you. Stay away from her, Ace. Or next time, you won't be able to walk away on your own."

"Please," Axel begged, sounding desperate. He turned to look at me. "Please..."

"Leave," Vale yelled as he blocked Axel's view.

I couldn't look away. The misery in Axel's voice made it difficult for me to ignore his pain. I watched as he stood with some effort. No one offered him a hand, and an awkward silence fell over the group.

He was defeated as he stumbled away. His shoulders were slumped, and his arms hung heavily by his sides. His face was slack with resignation when he looked back at us.

I didn't want to feel bad for him, but I did. He'd lost his best friend, and I could tell he was devastated. I didn't understand why he'd brought me into it, though. If he had regrets, it was only because of Vale, which was painful in its own right. He still didn't want me, but the idea of sharing a mate with his lifelong friend must have sparked something within him. It was yet another painful example of his disregard.

After hearing all the wonderful stories about Vale and the relationships he'd built with others, it was easy to guess what kind of loss this was for Axel. Sure, he had buddies here, but they were the same ones who laughed and egged him on when he was being a jerk. Even I knew those were friendships of convenience. Vale wouldn't have stood by as Axel belittled someone. He would have held Axel accountable, like he was doing now. He would have held him to a higher standard.

I'd barely known Vale a day, and I knew what Axel was losing. Even if I wanted to help prevent that, I couldn't. It wasn't my place. I would never make choices for my mate. If Vale didn't want to have anything to do with Axel because of what he'd done, then that was between them. I wouldn't take on that burden because it couldn't be mine to carry.

Vale had chosen me. He'd told me as such, but he'd also told me he couldn't be associated with someone who made the choices Axel had made, and I believed that had nothing to do with me. Regardless of my involvement, Vale would have questioned his connection to Axel. Even if Vale hadn't been my mate, he still would have been angry if he found out how Axel had been treating me. He wouldn't have been as invested, but definitely offended—like my friends were.

It wasn't until Axel was out of sight that Vale turned away from sentry duty and pulled me into him. "I'm sorry." He ducked his head down, breathing in my scent.

"It's not your fault. You have nothing to apologize for." I rested my head on his chest and hugged him. "You can't control him, and I don't expect you to."

"He shouldn't have said that."

"No, he shouldn't have."

He tightened his hold as the others talked around us, giving us a moment.

"Do you want to go or stay?"

"I'm okay to stay for a bit." I looked up at him. "If you are. We can go if that's what you want. I'm okay with either."

"No. He's not going to ruin our night. We'll leave when we're ready." He kissed me sweetly and sat me on his lap.

Sidric, Jed, and Brev gave him a bro-nod of approval and lifted their glasses. I knew they would have stepped in, but Vale hadn't given anyone the chance. Plus, he'd had it more than handled. Axel hadn't tried to fight or argue back, and he was drunk.

Puck walked over and held out his hand to Vale. "Welcome to the family, brother."

My eyes went wide. It was an innocuous statement. These guys always called each other "brother", and family could mean anything in a setting like this. Vale would join our school ranks in a few weeks and play for the Starball team next season. If anyone overheard, they wouldn't think twice about Puck's words. But we all knew his statement for what it was.

"Puck..." I whispered. I was in awe of his acceptance, and my voice cracked with emotion.

"It's all I can offer you for now, but I have plenty more for later," he said to both of us. His voice was quiet enough that no one would have heard, not even our friends or his mate a few feet away. "Tomorrow. Let's have a drink."

"I'd like that." Vale shook his hand. "Thank you."

"No, thank you. I—" Puck stopped mid-sentence, then grinned and shook his head as he released Vale's hand. "Fuck, it's really annoying sometimes." He laughed about the geas, and we all understood without further explanation. "Tomorrow," he repeated.

"Looking forward to it," Vale replied.

When Puck went back to his seat, Vale turned to me and smiled before kissing my temple.

As the evening wore on, Sidric, Jed, and Brev kept everyone entertained with their antics, and Puck joined in with his own brand of humor. Even Vale, who was still getting to know everyone, got in on the backchat.

Eventually, Vale and I said our goodbyes to the group and spent the rest of the night in each other's arms.

Chapter Seven

"Don't be nervous." I squeezed Vale's hand as we approached the private portal.

He snorted. "'Don't be nervous,' she says. We're just going to meet the Night Queen. No big deal."

I lifted on my tiptoes and kissed his lips. "Yes, but she's my mother first."

"I'll try to remember that."

We walked through the portal, and when we emerged on the other side, we found ourselves surrounded by my parents—like the last time I'd come home.

"There she is."

"Hi, pumpkin."

Pai and Baba pulled me into a hug between them.

"Hello, my darling," Papa, my Spring dad, said. My mother was tucked against him, and they pulled me into a joint hug next.

Father leaned over and kissed the top of my head before turning his attention to Vale, who hadn't moved.

When we all turned to look at him, he awkwardly dropped to one knee and bowed his head. "My Queen."

Mother chuckled and stepped forward to greet him. "It's alright, child. Stand."

He stood slowly but kept his eyes cast down. He was being courteous, but my mother wasn't stuffy about her requirements of subjects, at least not in private or with her family and friends. Sticking to the protocol in public was necessary, but even so, she was never unapproachable. Vale was purely respectful.

She held out her hand, and he didn't hesitate to clasp it. "Vale Wynman of the Summer Court house Wynman. It is an honor and pleasure to meet you and welcome you to my home."

"Night Queen Araphel, the honor is truly mine."

"We are overjoyed that our beautiful daughter has found her Summer mate. Allow me to introduce my Summer Knight, Elio." She turned and gestured to Pai, who stepped forward to meet Vale.

"Vale, welcome to our home. My name is Elio, formerly of the house Sulwens."

"It's a pleasure to meet you, Knight Lord."

"Call me Elio." Pai clapped Vale on the shoulder like they were old pals. "I'm just excited Summer didn't come in last place this time."

"It's not a game, Elio." Father stepped forward and introduced himself next. "I'm Noel, formerly of the Winter Court house Olwenn. We are glad to meet you."

Baba shouldered his way into the group and reached out. "It's an honor, Vale. I'm Lugh, formally of Autumn Court house Eembet."

Papa waited and introduced himself last. "And I'm Maxwell, formally of Spring Court house Ackland."

"It's a pleasure to meet you all," Vale said.

I leaned into Vale's side, and he wrapped his arm around my back instinctively like he'd been doing it for years. "What was that about Summer not coming in last? Are we talking about Starball?"

They all chuckled, but Pai explained, "No, not Starball, though I can see why you'd think that. You almost went to the championship, and you're quite the player. If the Day Court had you on their side, we might not have won the championship this year."

"Thank you. Puck deserved that win. Two years back-to-back is something to be proud of. I hope I can do the team justice next year."

"There's no doubt in my mind." Pai patted him on the back again. "I was talking about Summer not coming in last place as Lyra's mate. I was the last of Hesper's mates to reveal. It's sort of a running joke around here."

"Three years," my mother complained. "He made me wait three years. I believe I was the third longest geas-wearing princess in recent history."

"Better than Queen Olyta. She wore her geas for ten years before meeting her mates," Pai teased her.

"I don't mind it so much anymore." I shrugged. "It helps to have friends who know."

"Something to look into when you have a daughter of your own." Papa winked at me, and I blushed.

Father shook his head and pinched the bridge of his nose. "It's entirely too early for that, Maxwell. Don't scare the young couple."

"Yes, there are many years ahead of them before any of that matters." Mom's eyes crinkled with amusement looking at my two teasing dads. "The point is, we hope our Lyra will not have to wear her geas for long. And great Olyta met all of her mates on the same night, so the stars made up for her inconvenience."

"Now that two have presented themselves, I think it'll go fast," Pai said.

"Only one," Baba corrected.

"Yes, one that was worthy. We're unsure what the future holds in that regard," Father said as he led us through our family's private quarters of the castle to the dining room, where we would have brunch. "We've talked about it with the High Priestess, and we'll discuss it with you at a later date, but for right now, there's no need to sully this joyous occasion."

"Indeed," Mother agreed. "We want to hear everything about you, Vale. Lyra has told us very little. Perhaps you can start with your family?"

"I'd love to know what your tasks were that revealed Lyra to you so quickly. It is rather impressive to have it happen only hours after meeting," Baba mused.

"Yes." I folded my hands in my lap. "We'd known each other for less than half a day when my magic accepted him and the geas revealed me. Is that typical?"

"It's impressive. I wouldn't say it's typical—the process varies. Sometimes it's fast, but it can often take weeks or even months." Mother beamed at Vale. "You can't know how happy it makes me that she revealed to you so quickly."

"We're all thrilled," Father added as he pulled out my mother's chair. When she was settled, he signaled for the rest of us to take our seats.

"So, do you understand the tasks you passed?" Pai asked once we had all served ourselves.

We were doing a casual brunch, and no staff was allowed in the wing while Vale was here. The spell that kept my identity hidden would only go so far. Seeing a young fae couple with the Queen and her Knights would raise questions. It was better to keep prying eyes away.

"Yes. It's quite clear to me," Vale said. His eyes were guarded, but he reached out and took my hand. "I'm assuming Lyra didn't tell you that Axel and I grew up together?"

My parents froze, focusing on him.

Baba's voice was cautious as he said, "No, she did not."

Father looked at me pointedly before turning back to Vale. "She told us the bare minimum, it would seem."

Vale fidgeted in his chair, and my palms turned clammy under my parents' scrutiny. I hadn't told them, but not because I'd thought they'd treat Vale differently. I'd kept that information to myself so they wouldn't treat *me* differently. I didn't want to be handled like fragile glass anymore.

"Well, yes. Axel and I grew up together. Our parents were close when we were young, and we developed a friendship." Vale cleared his throat. "He was my best friend, and I considered him a brother. Even as toddlers, we were practically inseparable."

"You've known each other that long?" Mother's voice was high when she asked.

"I can't remember a time before we were friends."

"And now?" Father didn't take his eyes off Vale as he placed his napkin on his lap. "You speak in the past tense."

"That's because it is my past and not my future." Vale's voice was hard. "I heard the rumors about Spring Equinox. I won't go into details because, frankly, they no longer matter, but suffice it to say I always took Axel at his word and gave him my unflinching loyalty because of our friendship. I believed him when he denied what happened. It was unthinkable to presume otherwise."

Pai raised his brows. "He lied to you about it when you asked, then?"

"No." Vale shook his head. "I believed the statement the Spring Court and his family put out, but we never spoke of it. I was so sure it couldn't be true that I never asked him. I didn't want to disrespect him or question his integrity with such a ludicrous claim. If someone I thought of as a brother asked me if I'd done something so horrendous, I would have been offended. So I never brought it up, and he never said a word."

My mother took Father's hand. He would be the hardest of them all to mollify. He kept a cool head, but even with ice running through his veins, he was passionate—especially when it came to those he loved.

"We understand," my mother said. "I can appreciate why you'd refuse to believe such a thing."

"Thank you." Vale pulled in a breath and squeezed my hand before continuing. "After I met Lyra, I unknowingly introduced them to each other, but I knew something was off immediately. Afterward, I was told a disturbing story about my best friend and how his actions nearly killed my mate. I confronted him later that night, and he admitted the truth. I was shocked. As I've told Lyra, I chose her the instant I laid eyes on her. If I'd known what Axel had done... I don't want to speculate about what actions I might have taken, but I can't imagine supporting his side or trying to understand his motives. I still can't believe he did it half the time. It's surreal."

"It's practically unheard of," Father mused. I relaxed when he didn't question Vale or push him for more.

"After Axel told me everything, I knew the person I thought of as my best friend and brother was a stranger to me. His values and beliefs didn't align with my own. What he did was abhorrent, and I would have never been part of it. I had to let him go. I'd always given my loyalty to Axel in the past. I never questioned him or his motives. I thought we were the same. I thought our connection was so strong because we were best friends, but now I understand it was the mate bond. We weren't mated, but our connection to Lyra was always there. I didn't realize this at the time, but I'm convinced it's why I felt so drawn to him. Why I always chose him time and time again. So, when faced with that decision, when it really mattered, I chose Lyra."

My parents listened with rapt attention, and when Vale drew to the end of his story, Baba raised his brows. "There must not have been any hesitation in the decision."

"No, sir. None. It was my biggest task; the other tests pale in comparison to that."

"That must be why her magic revealed her to you so quickly then," Mother said. "There's nothing wrong with being an idealist, Vale. Just so long as you're practical as well. I believe you learned a valuable lesson that will serve you well as a Knight Lord in the future."

Father nodded. "Holding yourself to high standards and wanting those around you to do the same is admirable, but we are all fallible, and it's important not to be hypercritical of yourself or others. This sounds like a straightforward task, but as a perfectionist, I know it's not."

Vale grinned. "I'm learning that."

My mother's eyes glittered with tears. "After everything Lyra has been through, we're beyond grateful that she found someone who could help her trust in the mate bonds again. I would say you don't understand what that means to us or her, but as her mate and a member of her bond, you do."

"Painfully, yes," Vale agreed.

"And the other tests? What were they?" Pai leaned forward, questioning.

Vale drummed his fingers on the table. "This is going to make me sound like such a spoiled brat." He chuckled. "I've ... always gotten my way." He shrugged and flashed a sheepish smile.

"You're a noble son, so it kind of makes sense," Pai teased.

"That doesn't make it any less embarrassing." Vale shook his head. "The moment Lyra accepted me, I assumed she would follow me. I didn't ask or consider that she might want to stay at Araphel. I made that assumption, telling her she'd become a Hornets fan, and whether she realized it or not, I fully expected her to drop everything and move for me."

This was news to me. "I didn't get that from you at all."

"It didn't last long." He squeezed my hand. "Once I learned everything, I knew she needed her friends. Later that evening, I let her see a side of me I don't usually share."

"Humility and empathy are important qualities for a ruler, Vale." My mother gently arched her brows in approval.

"Well, we're happy to have you with us, Vale." Papa raised his glass. "Welcome to the family."

The sentiment was echoed by the rest of my parents.

With all the questions out of the way, we settled in for a relaxed meal as my parents took the opportunity to get to know my mate. We spent several hours chatting, and Vale's nerves quickly disappeared.

Puck and Roko arrived several hours later, followed shortly by the rest of my brothers. They all met Vale and promised to catch up with us after dinner.

After Shea shook Vale's hand, he turned to my parents. "I apologize for the interruption, but we need to pull you away from this. We've been informed of a concerning development."

Chapter Eight

Shea, Tunder, and Cleon served as advisors to the Queen in their official roles, making them deeply involved in all Night Court affairs. When my mother retired, they had the option to pursue their own paths as noble sons or continue their work on the council. Upon Puck's graduation at the end of the year, he would commence his internship in the Summer Court.

Following my mother's retirement, Shea and Tunder expressed their intention to assume positions on the council within their respective courts, occupying the seats once held by our dads' families. Shea would assume the role of the head of Olwen House in the Winter Court while Tunder would take charge of Eembet House in the Autumn Court.

As of right now, Cleon and Puck weren't interested in succession seats, but my parents weren't close to retiring, so that could change between now and then.

Even after I found all my mates and finally revealed myself to the realm, we'd have years of training ahead of us until it was time to take the reins.

"Speak freely," Father told Shea. "I know we've just met Vale, but he will be your sister's Knight Lord when she becomes Queen. They are privileged to whatever information you have, as it concerns them too."

I was as surprised as Vale to hear this. Of course, I'd been briefed on many things. I knew most of what my parents did, and I'd observed my mother for years while she worked. But to have Vale thrust into the fray so soon was unexpected.

"Yes, of course." Shea made eye contact with us, then turned back to my parents. "We've received an announcement about the formation of the New Night Coalition. What we've speculated is now confirmed. The New Day Consortium has expanded their rhetoric, and a syndicate in the Night Kingdom has become official."

"Do we know who organized it?" my mother asked.

"No. They are keeping everything as secret as the New Day group did. We don't have member numbers, names, or anything more than the invitation."

"How did we receive the invitation?" Father asked. "This makes little sense."

Shea lifted one corner of his mouth, revealing a dimple. "It came through the mail. It looks like we have an insider."

"An insider to a newly formed rebellion?" Baba leaned forward. "Well, that bodes well. If they have dissent in their ranks at the onset, then this can only be good for us."

"Take it with a grain of salt," Papa warned. "While an insider could provide valuable information, they may have their own agenda or hidden motives. We should tread carefully."

"Absolutely," Pai agreed. "Exercising caution is necessary, but if this communication is from a sympathizer, it could indicate that the presumed leaders of this group are not as widely accepted as they perceive themselves to be."

"The New Day's message wasn't received well in the Day Court, and the rebellion ended before it even began. Why would someone try the same thing here?" Vale asked.

"Unfortunately, this is something you will face quite often," Father told him.

"These are only the newest and most vocal rebel cells. Neither the Day nor the Night Queen of the realms control the flow of magic, as these traitors believe. We are not gatekeepers who decide who gets access to what magic. What you see is what you get. We are balanced, as you have been taught your entire life. But some believe if they sat at the top, they could amass more power for themselves," Baba explained. "And that's simply not true. Magic is a gift, and though we wield it, it chooses us. It's not sentient the same way you and I are, but it is perceptive in its own way. The Queen and her Knights are gifted—or cursed, depending on your view—with the responsibility of maintaining balance. While we hold more elemental power and magic, it's only for a time, and we share that burden with our counterparts in the Day Realm."

"It's our responsibility to keep people from abusing their position. Do you remember your magical history studies in prep school?" my mother asked Vale.

The story of how the Queen and her mates came into power is one I'd grown up hearing. The lesson taught in school was much the same, minus a gruesome detail or two.

A long time ago, before there was one Queen for each Kingdom, there were five rulers in each realm: Day, Night, Summer, Winter, Autumn, and Spring. Each seasonal court had a King, and the epoch of day and night had a Queen.

The four Kings constantly fought for power and control, waging wars across the realms, and they even joined forces in an attempt to take over the realms of Day and Night. Some seasonal courts fell to Kings who weren't fit to rule. The people suffered, as did the land. The disruption to the power balance depleted our magic. Fae died, animals suffered, forests burned, and cities and towns were leveled, leaving the citizens displaced.

The Queens stepped in time and time again to broker peace with treaties and alliances. Marriage and shared heirs were leveraged in an attempt to maintain balance. Sometimes it worked, and there was peace among the Kings and the realms, but it never lasted long. The Kings always wanted more.

Legend is that Magic herself eventually stepped in with help from the Deity of Fate and the Goddesses of Day and Night. They stripped the Kings of their power and imbued it into the only rulers who had ever cared and treated the realms with love and respect. From then on, the Queens of the Realms had the strongest connection to magic, holding power in all the seasons and the epoch of their court. They were granted sole reign, and the realms became kingdoms.

To ease the burden, the Queens were given mates from each seasonal court to maintain the balance and help her carry the load.

Mother told Vale the tale she'd told me many times before. "Since the dawn of the first Queens, there have been factions that want to take power and return to the old days. Knowing the history of war—and the peace we've enjoyed since—isn't enough to dissuade their ambition for power. It is our constant battle."

"Why would anyone want to disrupt the balance?" Vale shook his head. "It's obvious this is the best way. There is no suffering. The history is thoroughly accounted for and retold. It doesn't make sense why anyone would want to regress."

"Megalomania rarely makes sense." Baba shook his head. "Those consumed by this outlook cannot be reasoned with. They believe in the lies they tell themselves and others, despite the evidence to the contrary. All we can do is maintain the balance."

"The ranks we hold come with great sacrifice and responsibility, Vale, but none of us would have it any other way," Father said.

"It's not easy," Pai agreed, crossing his arms over his chest. "We've had to do things that none of us ever want to do again. But our job is vital for the realms and our people."

"How can we help?" I asked.

"You can't, not this time. You must watch and learn," Papa said.

"This is happening for a reason. It's no coincidence that this rebellion is becoming relevant now that you are receiving your mates. Perhaps this will be your bonds' task as a whole, to determine your readiness for your future responsibility," Father explained.

Mother tilted her head. "I believe that is the case. Each of you must prove yourselves to each other. The Knights, of course, undergo tests to determine their compatibility with the future Queen. Lyra has been tested her entire life, and in ways yet unknown, she is also being tested by accepting each of you," she said, looking at Vale. "But as a bond group who will one day rule this kingdom, you will have to prove you can preside justly so the people and realm never suffer. You must show each other and Magic herself that you can prosper."

"But how will we know?"

Her eyes sparkled with delight. "That's the trouble with the gift you've been given. We call it a burden for a reason, my love. There are never clear answers, and there aren't necessarily right or wrong ones either. You will learn as you go, and you won't understand much of it until it's over."

"Helpful, Mother." I smirked at her.

She winked. "We all had to do it. It only seems fair that you do too.

Father turned to Shea. "Do you know anything else? Is there a name or any other information on this invitation that could be helpful? Other than how it mysteriously dropped on our laps."

"Yes and no." Shea took a seat. "I probably should have led with this, but it was delivered with all other correspondence this morning and was labeled urgent. It caught our eye because it was addressed to Princess Araphel and Knight Lords."

"For crying out loud, son, why didn't you start with that?" Father shook his head. "It doesn't change the message, but it is something to go on."

Shea threw up his hands. "Sorry. I didn't know what we were comfortable saying in front of the new guy." He looked at Vale. "No offense."

"None taken, but now I'm more invested than I was thirty seconds ago." Vale sat up straight. "I made a promise to protect my mate, and I intend to keep it. If someone sent it to her specifically, it demands my attention."

His attentiveness was the hottest thing in all the realms, and it made me feel all warm and fuzzy inside. I held back a smile, but I couldn't hide my blush.

"Correct answer." Papa knocked on the table and gave him a nod. "What did the generals have to say?" he asked Shea.

The correspondence would have passed through our security team and the hands of the Night Court Guardians before ever reaching the family. Nothing entered this castle without going through rigorous inspection first.

"It caught our attention that the invitation was addressed to Lyra—or, more specifically, to the title she holds. It confirmed our suspicions about the existence of a rebel group."

"You're assuming the reference to Knight Lords indicates her mates? Does that mean they know she's found one?" Vale asked.

Tunder spoke up for the first time. "There's no way to know. I don't see how, but Lyra's presentation and the circumstances surrounding it haven't been as closely guarded as those before her."

My back straightened. "You think someone knows?"

He gave me his best comforting smile. "We don't know, Lala, but we shouldn't rule it out."

There was grumbling from my parents and brothers about his response, but I was quiet as I wondered how they could have discovered my identity. And if someone knew, what were they planning to do with the information?

"Forgive me," Roko interrupted. He'd been so quiet that I'd completely forgotten he was with us. "I apologize for my ignorance. I know there are reasons for hiding the princess until all her mates have found her and passed their tasks, but why is it so bad if she is discovered early? It wouldn't change who her mates are, would it?"

All of us turned to my parents for the answer. Mother smiled at him and looked at Baba to explain.

"Imagine if Axel had accepted the bond knowing who Lyra was, and she'd accepted it not knowing his true character," Baba said. My brothers, I, and Vale all tensed at the simple explanation. "If he'd been the way he was from the beginning but hid it from her until after they solidified the bond..." He shook his head. "There is a reason the magic tests us. From what I understand, he thinks he deserves the position he denied himself. He deserves the power and the title. But for what reason? What would he do with it? How would he have treated Lyra after he got what he wanted? How would he have interacted within the bond group once the others joined? There are a lot of variables to consider, and they all could have potentially disrupted the balance."

"When you first met Lyra, what did you notice?" Papa asked Vale.

Vale turned to me and scanned my face. "Honestly? Her. I know that's not a clear answer, but she was all I could see. Her eyes, her beautiful face. Everything else faded away. She was the only thing I could see."

My mother's shoulders relaxed as her eyes swam. "That's how it should be, dear. And what did you say to her?"

"Uh..." He glanced at me. "I don't know. I asked her to accept me, and I think I begged her for her name."

The table chuckled.

I took his hand and repeated his words to the group. "He said, 'By the goddess, I've found you. I've envisioned this day and dreamt of you nightly. Accept me, and I will spend the rest of my life making all your dreams come true.' He had to coax me a few more times because I was shocked and in disbelief after the last time. But then I told him my name, and now we're here."

Roko blushed, giving Puck a cheeky grin. "Wow, you Summer nobles must have romance and pretty words laced in your DNA."

My mother reached out and took Pai's hand. "I believe they do."

Pai winked at her and brought their linked hands to his mouth to kiss her knuckles.

Vale turned to me with a bright smile. "You remember?"

"I'll never forget."

His eyes twinkled as they flicked to my lips, but he leaned in and kissed my forehead instead.

Baba broke through the moment, dumping ice-cold water on me with his next question. "And what did Axel say?"

"Oh, I don't think I want to hear this," my mother whispered. "Lyra, you don't..."

Father took her other hand as he gave me an encouraging nod. "It's relevant to the question and the explanation."

Vale wrapped his arm around me, and I answered, "He asked me who I was and why I was there. When I told him I was nobody, he said, 'Exactly. You're weak. I can barely sense any magic from you at all. I'm a Spring Court noble. I can't be mated to a nobody female with weak magic.' He told me that the bond was nothing—he called it a thing. He said he'd find his true mate when the ceremony began and suggested that he was destined to be with the Night Princess. Then he demanded I leave so I didn't get in his way. He also told me not to attend future mating revelries."

The air in the room stilled, and the temperature lashed from hot to cold. I'd told them pieces of what Axel had said, but I'd never repeated his exact words to them.

Vale moved his chair back and lifted me onto his lap, holding me close.

"I had no idea," Father said, his voice low. "I'm so sorry, my daughter."

Mother wiped her eyes, and my dads shifted around as they struggled to decide whether they should comfort their mate or their daughter. In the end, they reached for her since Vale had me cocooned against his enormous body.

Roko sniffled from the other side of the table. "I'm so sorry. I should have kept my mouth shut."

"It's alright," I said, shifting around to look at him.

"Fuck, Lyra, I wish you'd stop saying that," Puck ground out through his teeth. "It's not alright. It's never been alright."

"It doesn't matter anymore. We need to move on." I looked at my parents. "Please, continue."

Baba focused on Roko, who was wiping his eyes with his napkin. "Axel only cared about her power and what he thought she offered him. He didn't see her. Lyra's very essence is hidden in the geas for this purpose. Her magic is dimmed, her appearance is changed, and her ability is obscured. Her glamour is not unique or powerful enough to draw attention."

"Yes," Roko said, nodding and looking at Vale. "The difference is very clear. I understand now. As painful as it was for you and your bond, I understand why it's necessary. I couldn't imagine you being tied to someone like that."

"Holy shit!" Vale sat up and everyone startled at his exclamation. "It's Axel!" he stated and looked around the room as if waiting for everyone to agree.

"You're gonna have to explain further, big guy." Puck raised his brows at my mate. "We just met. We don't understand your shorthand yet. What's Axel?"

"The New Night group. Well, maybe not Axel himself," Vale said. "It could be his family—or his dad, more specifically. He's been pushing for more power and vying for a higher position on the council for years, as far as I know. Even my parents stopped associating with him because of the views he held. I'd bet my Starball trophies that Axel's dad is part of this New Night Coalition. Hell, he may even be the leader."

"That actually makes some sense." Baba looked at my other parents and brothers. "He has been getting more comfortable speaking out at meetings and bringing up topics that align with what the New Day rebellions platformed on."

"Yes, he has made some off-handed remarks about the past and how the realms were ruled long ago," Papa said.

Shea turned to Vale. "You believe Axel could be part of this?"

Vale pulled in a deep breath. "I do. I hate to say it, but the person I knew or thought I knew..." He looked at me and tightened his hold. "He wouldn't have rejected his mate or done those awful things to Lyra. But the person he is, the one he became while I wasn't paying attention, is different. I don't know who he is anymore. But I know they are his father's views and would reason that they are his views now, too."

Shea turned to Tunder, then Tunder looked at Cleon.

Cleon leaned on the table and focused on Vale. "We have a proposition for you."

Chapter Nine

"You can't ask him to do that!" Puck stood and threw his napkin on the table. "You know what she's been through. There has to be another way."

"If Vale's right, he's our best shot!" Shea yelled back at him.

"You think we don't know what we're asking? We know, Puck," Tunder argued. "We have mates too. And Lyra's our sister. We understand what we're asking."

When my parents didn't say anything, Puck turned on them. "You're not seriously considering this? After everything?"

"Sit down," Father ordered. His face was as hard as ice, but my brothers complied immediately.

Puck flopped in the chair. "This is bullshit." He lifted his glass, draining it in one gulp.

"Puck," Pai said in a placating tone. "Calm down."

"No one would ever ask you to do something like this if you were uncomfortable," Baba told Vale. "Take some time to think about it. Rekindling your friendship to gain his trust would be the first step in a long game."

"I'll do anything to keep Lyra safe. I'm not sure how I would manage this, though." Vale looked around the table. "I ended our friendship, our association—everything. I cut him off."

"And beat the shit out of him," Puck added. "Which he deserved but still isn't enough."

"Son, please," Mother chided him and then looked back to Vale. "Obviously, if we were to consider using you as a way to infiltrate this group, there would be a lot to go over. We're also assuming Axel and his father are a part of this. I agree, it seems likely, but it's all speculation."

"And what better way to get confirmation than by using the one person we have on the inside," Tunder said. "If we're wrong, we've put Vale through a series of uncomfortable encounters and conversations. But if we're right..."

"I don't want to agree, but I do," Roko said, and Puck practically broke his neck looking at his mate.

"What?" he hissed.

"I'm sorry, but they're right. If I could do it, I would, but Vale said they were like brothers. If Axel's going to trust anyone, it's Vale. He's the best shot at getting answers. Think of how this will protect Lyra."

"I am thinking of that," Puck argued. "I don't want her hurt, and putting her in that asshole's proximity will hurt her!"

"No." Vale shook his head. "If I do this, Lyra won't be part of it. I won't do that to her. You'll only use me."

"Agreed," Shea said as the others nodded.

"I also won't leave her." Vale looked around the room. "I don't know what you're thinking, but if it involves me staying away from her, I won't do it. I won't play any role that makes me appear at odds with her."

"Of course not." Shea leaned forward, dismissing the idea. "We would never ask that of you, or her, especially after everything. You'll just have to convince him you've had a change of heart, and are willing to give him a second chance and make amends. Once you've earned his trust again, we can strategize and determine the best way to get information about the group and his involvement without causing suspicion."

"We understand the delicate nature of this situation," Cleon added, nodding in support. "Rekindling a broken friendship can be challenging, but it may be the key to unlocking the information we need. It will take time and effort, and you'll need to convince him you genuinely care and are willing to forgive his past grievances."

Tunder leaned back, his expression thoughtful. "While you work on rebuilding the friendship, we'll keep digging and try to discover who the sender was. But we're here to support you every step of the way, and it's your call on how to handle him. If you're up for it," he assured, his tone conveying the seriousness of the matter.

"This is a lot," Baba said. "Take a few days to think it over. Contrary to what the Night Dukes would have you believe, there's no rush. There isn't an ax hanging over your head for a decision."

"No, just an Ax*el*," Puck grumbled.

I snorted, and he smirked up at me.

"Lyra and I will discuss it," Vale told them.

Shea and Tunder bumped knuckles at his answer, and Cleon gave me a wink. They were the Queen's advisors, but they were my brothers first. Their silly gestures and poorly timed jokes never stopped.

"In the meantime," Papa said. "I've expedited your transfer. Consider it our gift to you. Welcome to the family."

Vale perked up. "You're shitting me! I thought it would take weeks."

Mother laughed. "There are perks to having a school named after your family line."

"You don't have to use the mated suite until you're ready, but one has been set aside for you two. Until then, you also have a dorm room of your own," Papa said. "Both are move-in ready. You'll need to visit administration for your schedule, and you're all set."

Vale's smile was like the sun. It spread across his face and lit up the room. "Well, what do you think, my mate?"

I blushed. "I think we should talk about that later."

"Eh, just get it over with. Don't make him move twice," Puck said, letting out an *oof* when Roko elbowed him playfully in the gut.

"Leave them be. They practically just met," Roko whispered.

"Pft, so? They already solidified the bond. What's left?" Puck grumbled, but it was all for show since his eyes sparkled with mirth.

Tunder shrugged. "That's true. They're stuck together forever now."

"Literally," Cleon added helpfully.

I groaned and dropped my head onto Vale's shoulder. "You guys are so embarrassing."

Vale chuckled.

"We have one last thing to discuss before we leave you for the night." Father pulled our attention back to him. "Winter Solstice."

Vale's brow wrinkled, and my mother noticed his confused expression. "Now that Lyra has been presented to court, part of her duty is to attend each official mating revelry until all of her mates reveal."

"You weren't at the Autumn Ceremony, though, or we would have met," Vale said, looking at me.

I sighed. "No. I should have been, but after Spring—"

"Shit," he cut me off. "Of course. I should have known."

"We thought it best she had some time after everything, and we weren't sure if she'd even attend Winter, but now that she's met you" — Mother looked at me hopefully — "we don't think you should put it off."

I agreed, though not very enthusiastically. "Alright."

Vale kissed my head, then turned to my parents. "How does it work? Can I go? Do I have to stay behind and wait to hear from someone?"

"It'll work like anyone else looking for their mates. Everyone has a pretty good idea of how many mates they have once one has been found. Lyra should have four minimum—you should be able to feel that now that you're bonded," Baba told him.

I looked at Vale, and he raised his hand to his chest. "I can feel it. I didn't pay much attention to it because I've been focusing on her, but now that you mention it, I feel the space that needs to be filled within her."

"Is it still three, Lyra?" Papa asked.

I nodded. "Yes. That's what it feels like."

"There's a different Spring mate, then?" Puck asked. "That's what that means?"

Everyone was quiet. There was no way to know. "Until the bond with Axel is completely severed, I don't know how to be sure," I mumbled. The space he should have filled was still tied to him, even if the connection was weak.

"We'll cross that bridge when we get to it. Let's stay positive and move forward," Father told us. "You'll attend together. We will be there as well. Since everyone knows you're friends with Puck and Roko, you can interact with them openly. But as for the rest of us, you won't indicate that you know us. You'll simply attend, dance, mingle, and go through the ceremony like any other."

"You have a couple of weeks before then. That should give you plenty of time to discuss everything we've dumped on you tonight," Pai said as he stood, and the others followed his lead. "But we're always here and available to you, Vale. You're part of this family. If you have questions or concerns, bring them to our attention. It's part of your job, which you'll begin training for soon." He smirked, and I felt Vale tense under me.

"Don't scare him off, Elio." Father shook his head as he held out a hand for my mother. "Let them settle into their bond before you initiate him into Knighthood."

"You're welcome to stay the night or return to the academy," my mother said after giving us hugs.

When they left, I said goodbye to my brothers. As much as they wished to get to know Vale, I was tired and wanted to go back to my dorm. We made plans for another time and left with Puck and Roko.

When we returned to Araphel, Vale walked me to my room, stopping at the entrance as I opened my door.

"Are you coming in?"

"Only if you're sure," he said casually, but I could see the hope in his eyes.

"Of course I'm sure. It's why I wanted to come back here. We should talk about everything."

"I thought you were tired."

"I am, but not so tired that I don't want to spend time with you." I felt my cheeks grow warm at the admission.

"Thank fuck." He pulled me into his arms and closed the door behind him. "I don't want to be away from you right now, either."

He crushed his mouth against mine hungrily. I couldn't help but giggle at his enthusiasm, which twisted into a needy moan when his tongue met mine.

Vale sat on the couch and pulled me across his lap. I indulged myself with his lips for a while longer before I sat back so we could talk. "If you want to help discover who's behind the New Night Coalition, I think you should."

He reached for my hand and kissed my knuckles. "I won't do anything that makes you uncomfortable."

"I don't want you to do anything based on how you think it will affect me. My brothers are right in that it will help us and our future. If we can eliminate the problem now, while my parents are in charge and with my brothers' help, that will be better for us in the long run. Someday we'll take over, and I don't want to be dealing with this years later."

He sighed and looked around the room. "I don't know how to get past what Axel did, even if I'm only faking a relationship with him. I don't think he'd even believe it at this point."

"He went out of his way to find us at the party. I think it's a good sign that he will at least hear you out."

Vale sighed. "I agree. We need to stop these traitors, and if we can learn anything through Axel, I'll do it. But the second I know what he has to offer on the subject, I'm done."

"You can go to my family for guidance, but you'll be in complete control of the situation."

"Good." He tugged me closer. "Let's stop talking about this for now. Will you come to High Crest with me tomorrow to pack up my things? My parents are traveling, so I can't introduce you yet, but my sister and her mates will be there. Would you like to meet them?"

"I'd love to meet your sister, Vale. Yes, I will go with you." I wrapped my hands around his face.

His shoulders relaxed, and he turned his head to kiss my inner wrist. "We can get my room figured out in the morning before we go. One of my sister's mates has Affliction for Divination Magic. He has teleportation and telekinesis abilities so he can transport my things into my room for me."

"You mean into our room," I told him definitively. My mind was made up.

His eyes flashed, and a slow smile tipped his lips. "Really?"

"Don't ever tell Puck, but I think he's right. Why wait? Why put it off? You're mine, and I'm yours, and I never want to be apart. Let's move into the mated dorms."

"What if I snore?"

"You do snore, but that doesn't change anything. I still want to live with you."

He laughed as he tickled my sides. "I don't snore."

"Yes, you do." I giggled and squirmed. He stopped when I straddled his lap. "Just a little, and it's adorable." I bent and kissed his lips.

"Adorable, huh?" He pulled my bottom lip into his mouth and let it go with a pop. "Tell me more."

I ran my hands over his broad shoulders, trailing them down his muscled chest. "Your skin feels like it was warmed by the sun." I pushed his shirt over his head. "You're so hot." The double meaning wasn't lost on him as his eyes lit up.

"Are you hot for me?" He pressed kisses down my neck while lifting my shirt.

I panted when he flung the garment to the other side of the room. "Yes."

We kissed with tongue and teeth, pulling and nipping at each other as our mouths came together. He unclasped my bra, freeing my breasts before undoing my pants. When the zipper was down, he lifted me and carried me to my room.

When my feet touched the floor, I kicked off my shoes and shimmied out of my clothes. With both of us naked, we moved to the bed, but before he could join me on the mattress, I grabbed his cock at the base and took him in my mouth.

He groaned at the contact and threaded his hands into my hair, letting me control the pace. He was so big that my mouth stretched as wide as possible. His skin was soft, warm, and silky smooth, and I hummed in delight at his taste.

"You look so pretty with my cock in your mouth," he grunted as his thigh flexed under my free hand. "Ah, yes..." His hand tightened in my hair when I took him down my throat and swallowed. "Fuck, Lyra, that feels so good." He ground himself into me before pulling out of my mouth. "Someday soon, I'll let you suck me off, but I need to be inside you right now."

Like I weighed nothing, he spun me around and positioned me on my hands and knees at the foot of the bed. Urging my legs apart, he pushed my shoulders down and ran his palm along my spine. When he reached my ass, he grabbed my cheeks with both hands and spread me open to expose my sex.

"Such a pretty little pussy." He hummed as he swept his thumb from my clit to my entrance, dipping it inside. Then he moved the pad up and circled my tight ring with my silky arousal. "You'll let me in here someday too, won't you, beautiful?" he crooned as he slowly pushed his thumb inside, stimulating me with gentle pumps.

I groaned, swaying into his thumb as I throbbed with anticipation.

"That's a good girl," he praised, and when his thumb was all the way in, he notched the head of him against me and slid into my core.

Wrapping his free hand around my hip, he rocked me back and forth on his hot flesh as he worked his thumb in and out of my tight hole, slowly building momentum. We were loud, and with the added stimulation of his thumb, I didn't last long. Soon, I was clenching and pulsing around him as my orgasm swept over me.

"That's it, Princess, come on my cock," he panted, moving his free hand around to play with my clit. Vale kept up his rhythm until I came again, then he removed his thumb, grabbed onto my other hip, and held me in place, pounding into me to finish himself off.

When he pulled out of me, I collapsed on the bed from exhaustion. He carried me to the shower, and afterward, I curled against him in bed and promptly fell asleep on his shoulder.

Chapter Ten

"Welcome to High Crest Academy, Princess," Vale whispered in my ear.

High Crest Academy was a sprawling campus full of white marble buildings with gold-plated domes and intricate mosaics along the walls, depicting all things Summer and epitomizing the court.

The hunter-green iron gates at the main entrance were covered in ornate carvings of sunflowers and flanked by two majestic statues of phoenixes with wings lit by eternal flames to represent the first Summer Knight, Lord High Crest.

The academies in both kingdoms paid homage to the founding rulers of the realms, and while I was biased toward Araphel, there was something unique and special to love about each premier school.

Through the gates, a grand courtyard extended out to the crystal-clear waters of the sea, framed by a white sand beach. Fountains sprayed ocean mist into the warm summer air, and lush gardens perfumed the breeze with the sweet smell of fruits and flowers.

The main building of the academy was a towering structure with an open-concept ground floor that allowed the students to enjoy the sunshine, fresh air, and scenic views. The upper floors were dedicated to classrooms, each with balconies and large windows overlooking the courtyard and beach.

Much like Araphel and the other academies, the dormitories were divided into various elements, each featuring a unique theme symbolizing the corresponding element and court. Vale's Imperium Magic was fire, which was obvious given his shifted form as a dragon, but he also possessed elemental magic related to air.

"I'm on the top floor." He pointed to the highest level of the fire elemental dorm. Like most other buildings, it was surrounded by a large balcony overlooking the ocean.

I yelped in surprise and wrapped my arms around Vale's neck as he lifted me into his arms. "What are you doing?" I asked with a giggle.

"Giving you a ride." He winked.

Suddenly, two massive wings tore through his shirt. I knew he could partially shift, having seen his tail at the party the other night, but seeing his dragon wings stretch behind him was nothing short of majestic.

They were an iridescent shade of red, and as I ran my fingers over the leathery membrane, I was surprised to discover they were soft to the touch.

"They're so beautiful."

Vale tightened his hold on me, and a low groan rumbled through his chest. "Lyra..." He dropped his head to my shoulder and shuddered. His hot breath spilled over me as he whispered, "That feels amazing."

"Has no one touched you here before?"

One of the strongest males I'd ever met was trembling beneath my fingers. I marveled at the power I held with a simple touch, desperate to see what other sounds I could draw from my mate.

"No." He panted when I wrapped my hand around the leading edge of one wing and stroked it gently like I would his cock. "No one else."

"You denied yourself? Why?"

"Some things are sacred, and I only wanted to experience them with my mate." He flicked his tongue out to taste my neck before pressing hungry kisses up my throat. "I've never allowed anyone to touch me like this. Just like I've never carried anyone. You will be the only one I hold these memories with, Lyra."

My eyes blurred, and happy tears slipped down my cheeks as I pressed my lips to his. "You are perfect. Take me up. Right now, Vale." I ran my tongue across his bottom lip before kissing his jaw.

"Yes, my Queen," he whispered, launching us off the ground.

I wanted to enjoy the view, and someday I knew I would, but right then, I needed to please my mate. Luckily, I was wearing a skirt.

"Higher," I whispered in his ear as I tightened my hold around his neck and shifted my legs to his waist.

Vale helped me straddle him as he soared into the air well past the dorms, high enough in the sky that there was no hope of us being seen. Reaching between us, I pulled the crotch of my lace panties to the side while Vale held my legs and undid his pants simultaneously.

"You're making so many of my fantasies come true today."

With my skirt pushed up around my waist, we both watched as I slid myself onto him. When he was fully seated, I tightened my legs around him and circled my hips as I rode him. Between keeping us in the air and managing his pleasure, Vale was at a loss for words. He merely grunted and moaned between breathy pleas as he said my name. The angle of my position—and the exhilaration of riding my dragon mate in the sky—spiked my pleasure quickly, and I could sense through our bond that Vale was close.

Reaching out, I stroked his wings and tightened myself around him and was rewarded with a dragon's roar as Vale tipped over into orgasm. His hot release was so strong that I felt him spurt inside me, and his enjoyment became my own as I clenched on him with a climax of my own.

We may have evaded attention before, but I wasn't so sure that was the case now. Vale's voice carried, echoing over the campus below. When the pleasure waned and I could focus again, I found myself caught in his heavy gaze. He stared at me in wonder, much like he did when we'd first laid eyes on each other, then he crushed his mouth to mine.

"You are utterly exquisite," he mumbled between kisses.

I hummed against his lips. "Was it everything you hoped for?"

"Better." He nuzzled my neck. "So much fucking better. You're perfect—my perfect mate in every way, Lyra."

Using my water magic, I cleaned us up as we laughed and struggled to right our clothes. It was good that I wasn't afraid of heights, or I might have been terrified. But I trusted Vale with my life, and even if he dropped me, I could shift in to my Nightshade form and fly myself to safety.

"Promise me one thing," Vale said once my arms were wrapped around him again.

"Anything."

He beamed. "Next time we do this, promise me you'll be naked so I can lay you out on a bed of wind as I take you."

"Only if it's dark." I smirked. "And only if you're naked too."

He jerked against me as I trailed a finger over his wing.

"Deal. Now hold on, Princess." He tucked his wings, leaned forward, and sent us into a nosedive toward the dorms.

I wanted to scream, but instead, I laughed as my belly flipped with excitement. Just when it seemed like we were too close to stop, his wings snapped out. We landed without a hitch, and instead of putting me down, he continued forward with me in his arms until we were at his dorm.

There were voices inside, and when Vale walked into the room, we were met by two burly men and a tiny woman. The men argued while playing a battle game on a console, and the woman ran her fingers through their hair. They were sitting on the floor in front of her while she was cross-legged on the couch, laughing at their banter. When we walked in, she spun around so fast that the two men jumped to attention as if to defend her from an attack.

"Finally! We've been waiting for an hour." The woman clapped and rushed to jump over the couch. "This is her?" she asked Vale, then looked at me. "You're you."

I giggled and squirmed in Vale's arms until he let me down.

"I'm Lyra." I held out my hand.

Her ash-blonde hair cascaded down to her waist, framing a face adorned with sparkling green eyes. The softness of her features radiated delicate beauty while her wide smile exuded warmth and joy. Though shorter in height, she possessed a captivating presence that drew attention. The striking resemblance between her and Vale was impossible to miss. From their similar physical traits to their beaming expressions, Vale's sister was a feminine carbon copy of him, emanating the same dazzling charm.

"I'm so happy to meet you." She threw her arms around me, and because she was more petite, I huffed out a breath as I bent unexpectedly at the waist.

"Harlow!" Vale complained, but she ignored him and squeezed me tighter.

"Oh, hush, brother," she chided him before pulling back to greet me. "I'm Harlow, your new sister." She grinned, and I was convinced that sunshine ran through their veins. They both had smiles that made you feel warm.

Harlow took my hand and pulled me into the room to stand in front of her two burly mates. They both had dark hair, brown skin, and thick but well-groomed beards. They weren't as large as Vale, but they were built. "These are my mates and your brothers-in-law, Clive and Rogan."

"Hello."

"Hi."

They both greeted me politely but didn't reach out to shake my hand. They were stiff, nodding to Vale before focusing on their mate.

Her grin reached her eyes, and she blew them a kiss. "My guys are Kodiak shifters and have strict pack instincts about others that aren't their mates or blooded relatives. They're shy now, but give them time to know you, and we'll all be great friends."

"I understand." I smiled and gave them space by taking a step back. Vale was closer than I'd realized, and he placed his hand on my hip when I bumped into him.

Pack shifters were notoriously territorial, and while they didn't keep to themselves or stay out of society, they typically preferred to socialize within their groups.

"I'm taking that game with me." Vale's chest rumbled against my back as he teased his brothers-in-law.

Rogan whacked Clive on the chest playfully. "I told you."

"Who are you going to play with?" Clive raised his brows at Vale. "You'll be too busy with your new mate for video games."

"Lyra will play with me," Vale announced, and I looked up at him in surprise.

"I don't know how to play." I wrinkled my nose. I'd much rather garden or read a book than play a video game. "But I suppose I could learn." I shrugged.

Harlow practically swooned. "That's so sweet." Her green eyes twinkled, and she looked on the verge of tears. "She has no desire at all to play, but she's willing to try for you."

My eyes widened with her admission, and Vale chuckled before kissing the top of my head. "Harlow's Divination Magic is in Psyche, like yours. She's a telepath."

Harlow rolled her eyes and shook her head. "He makes it sound like I can read your mind. That's not how it works for me. I can sense an impression of your thoughts. It's not always clear, and I'm still learning."

"So you didn't hear that I would rather grow a vegetable garden than make cartoons kick each other in the head?"

Vale belted out a hearty laugh, and even Harlow's mates chuckled at my description of their game. I was teasing them, but that's what it looked like they were doing when we'd walked in.

Harlow's face softened with affection as she watched her brother's joy. She turned to me. "No, I didn't hear that specifically, but I sensed that you were thinking about plants. Which makes sense," she said, glancing at the green Elemental Magic bracelet on my wrist. "Clive's secondary magic is in Earth, isn't it, babe?" She turned toward him with a playful grin.

"Yes, baby." He bent down and kissed her lips. Then he cleared his throat and gave me another nod before looking at Vale. "Do you want me to send this shit right away, or are you hanging a bit?"

"He's hanging," Rogan said, turning back to the TV and picking up his controller. "If he wants to take this game from us, he can play me for it."

"We don't have time for games."

"Yes, we do." I turned in Vale's arms and cut off his denial. "We can stay for a while, and I can watch you play."

"And I can teach her what she needs to know to kick your ass later." Harlow clapped her hands and then jumped—literally—from where she was to the couch. "Come sit next to me, sister." She waved her hand to the space beside her and flopped down on the cushion.

Clive took his place by her feet next to Rogan, and Vale joined them on the floor. I settled on the cushion behind him so I could sit by his sister. She spent the next hour telling me about the game. I wouldn't call it teaching since I didn't play, and I'd probably forget everything she told me when we left, but it was fun anyway. Soon, the three men were bantering as they took turns with the console. Harlow was chatty and commanded most of the conversation, which I was grateful for. I was still getting used to interacting with people on such a personal level. I felt a little awkward sometimes, but with Harlow taking control of the situation, I felt at ease. I answered all her questions about myself and told her what I could about my magic and abilities. While we both possessed Psyche Divination Magic, her telepathy was much different that my Astral Projection.

From her, I learned that although her mates were not blood-related, they were often mistaken as brothers due to their resemblance and close relationship. They'd grown up together and had been revealed as Harlow's mates at the same time during a town festival. She also told me her shifted form was a Kitsune, which explained why she was so agile. Kitsune were cunning, and though her animal form wasn't as formidable as Vale's, they shared a strong affinity for fire.

Harlow was as open and warm as Vale, and though her mates were reserved, they didn't seem to mind how close I was as we sat together. They even answered my questions about the game when I asked. I took that as a positive sign. I understood their culture and knew it wasn't directed at me personally, so I was grateful they were already warming up to the idea of me in their lives.

"Alright, fine, you can keep the damn game." Vale playfully punched Rogan in the arm. "Think of it as payment for being my mover."

"So, now I'm a pack mule? That's fucked up, dude."

"What else are brothers for?" Vale tilted his head as if deep in thought.

"I'm keeping the game because you're an ass, not for payment." Rogan smirked and took the controller from Vale.

"I'll miss you too, buddy." Vale reached up and tousled his hair.

Rogan laughed and backed away from him. "Where do you want your stuff? Or should I deliver it to the middle of the lake at Araphel?"

"They're always like this—you'll get used to it," Harlow whispered as she linked her arm around mine.

"I like it."

Vale heard me and turned to give me his big smile.

"You can send it here," Vale told Rogan, giving him the coordinates for our mated room. My stuff had already been taken earlier today. "And make it snappy, mule. I have a mate to feed."

"So do we," Clive added, coming over to stand next to Harlow.

She pulled me into another unexpected hug before tucking herself under Clive's arm. "I'm so happy to have met you, Lyra. We'll visit when you get settled, and you can give us a private tour of the Queen's Academy. Oh, maybe for taco night! I hear you have the best taco night."

"It is pretty amazing," I admitted.

"Then it's a date," she announced.

Rogan evanesced Vale's things to our dorm, and we said our goodbyes as they left.

Vale stalked over to me after closing the door. "There's this cute little bistro downtown I'd like to take you to."

"What do they serve?" I asked. "I am pretty hungry after our earlier activities."

Wrapping his hands around my face, he tilted my head and kissed me, his warm breath teasing my lips as he said, "I'm pretty hungry for more of those activities. Maybe Rogan left the bed."

"We didn't need a bed earlier."

He chuckled and pressed his lips to mine, kissing me sweetly. "How about you let me take you to dinner, and after, I get you for dessert?"

"I like dessert."

"And I like—"

A knock on the door interrupted the conversation, which was quickly turning into foreplay.

"We'll pick this up later." He patted my bottom and stood to his full height.

"We have forever."

"Yes, we do." He winked at me, then went to the door. "What did you forget, Rogan? Your pride? I won those games fair…" Vale trailed off, and his posture went rigid.

He was so large that his body hid whomever was on the other side of the door, but it didn't take me long to connect the dots.

"What the hell are you doing here, Axel?" Vale snapped.

Chapter Eleven

"Vale," I murmured.

He twisted to look over his shoulder, and Axel's eyes widened when he caught sight of me. I turned my focus to my mate and gave him the tiniest smile.

Vale sighed and closed his eyes, facing his former friend again. "Axel, we were just getting ready to leave. This is going to have to wait," he said in a slightly friendlier tone.

"I didn't know she'd be with you."

"She's my mate," Vale snapped. "She'll always be with me."

"That's not what I meant." Axel's voice was quiet and subdued. "I just wanted to talk. I didn't think she'd moved here yet."

"Moved here?" Vale shook his head. "What are you talking about?"

"I heard you were getting ... a-a mated room," he stuttered. "I wanted to talk to you before you moved in together."

"Who told you... Never mind. It doesn't matter. Look, this isn't a good time. We've had a long day, and I'd like to feed my mate and take her home. I'll find you when we get back to campus. We can talk there."

Vale went to close the door, but Axel's hand hit the wood. "What do you mean 'back on campus'? You mean here, right?"

"No. Back on *our* campus. At Araphel, where we all attend."

"You can't!"

"And why the fuck not, Ace?" Vale growled.

"Because it's not..." His words seemed to get stuck in his throat. "You know why, Vale," he whispered.

"What do I know, Axel?" Vale took a step forward. "Tell me. Explain it to me like I'm five."

"It's what's best for her," Axel said, even quieter than before. I wasn't sure if he was trying to keep me from listening or if I had a hard time hearing because of the rumbling coming from my dragon mate.

"And what the fuck would you know about what's best for her?"

I put my hand on Vale's back, and he froze. He was hot to the touch, and a vibration rattled his bones as he attempted not to shift. The skin on his neck and arms was shimmering and transforming into red leathery scales. When he looked at me, the golden rings of his dragon form were also present.

"Mate," he rumbled, his deep voice rattling through the room. Even though it was terrible timing, the claim made me melt a little inside.

"Yes, yours," I told him.

Reaching up, I ran my finger over his jaw where ridges were rising. He hummed at the touch and visibly relaxed enough that his dragon form receded.

My hand fell to his chest, and I patted his shirt. "I can go and—"

"No," Vale and Axel said at the same time.

I wasn't surprised Vale had refused, but I was taken aback that Axel had spoken up. Vale must have been surprised, too, because he raised a brow, and we both looked at Axel.

"What I meant to say is..." Axel said, looking at me apologetically before focusing on Vale. "I will go. I shouldn't have come here. I'm sorry." He held his hands up and backed away before turning to leave.

We watched him get halfway down the hall before Vale called out to him, "We'll have that talk later, Ace."

Axel's shoes squeaked on the floor, he stopped so fast. "Okay." His tone was questioning, but he nodded and left without another word.

Before the door was fully closed, Vale wrapped his arms around me protectively, squeezing me and breathing deeply at my neck. "This is going to be harder than I thought," he confessed after a few moments.

"You did well."

"I didn't." He shook his head. "He had no right to talk about you like that."

"Set ground rules. Just because you'll do this and act like you've forgiven him doesn't mean you can't have boundaries. He may even become suspicious if you don't."

Nodding, he released me. "That's true. I'll tell him he can't speak about you at all. You'll be completely off-limits."

"That's a great idea," I said, brushing his hair away from his face. "Now, let's go eat and forget about this for tonight."

Vale looked around the room one last time to make sure nothing was left behind, and then we left the dorm. It was early evening, and the fireflies were out with the aphid moths and pixies. The sun was setting over the ocean, sparkling off the rippling water and casting a dreamy haze over the realm. A warm breeze carried the sweet smell of flowers through the balmy air. It was nice and cozy here, and if we didn't have to get back, I would have liked to stay.

As if he could read my mind, Vale said, "When my parents return, we'll spend a couple of days, and I will take you to my favorite spots."

He couldn't hear my thoughts—not really, anyway. Once our mate circle was complete, he'd be able to sense my emotions more clearly. And depending on the gifts the others brought with them, we could potentially gain the ability to send mental messages.

"I'd like that very much." I wrapped my arms around his waist, and he tucked me under his arm as we walked.

We were nearing the gates when another familiar voice echoed across campus. "You can drop the superiority act. I didn't mean to, and I've already been punished," Jana hissed.

"Not nearly enough," Axel snapped. "I told you to leave me alone. Now, fuck off."

"You don't get to dismiss me, Axel! Our parents want us to go together."

"I don't care."

The closer we got to the exit, the slower I moved. I hadn't realized it at first, not until Vale looked down at me questioningly.

"Why are you acting like this? You didn't seem to care before, and I already told you I didn't try to kill the stupid bitch! How was I supposed to know she was allergic to honey?"

Vale's jaw clenched at her words, and he tightened his hold.

"I told you never to speak about her—"

Axel's words cut off as we came into view. He stared us down while Jana ranted, speaking over him.

"You're such an asshole. Meira was right—you do want her. Well, too bad she's mated now, Axel! You should have fucked her when you had the chance."

Axel's face pinched with rage, and he glared down at her. His eyes darted toward us, and Jana glanced over her shoulder.

"Oh," she snarked, crossing her arms over her chest. "Figures you'd be the reason he's here. Well, I may as well apologize to your face. Then maybe I can go back to Araphel instead of slumming it at Valley Hill."

The Spring Court Academy was as beautiful as the rest of the realms' premier schools, so her attitude didn't make sense.

"You won't be returning there," Vale growled. "Ever."

"Whatever, Wynman." Jana rolled her eyes. "Our families are equal on the council, so it's not up to you. Speaking of, are your parents disappointed you mated a nobody? You had such potential. No offense." She smirked at me. "Oh, and sorry for accidentally almost killing you, *honey*."

Vale tried to shift me behind him, but I held my ground. I appreciated his protectiveness, and if I was in danger, I'd want him by my side. But I didn't need him to fight my battles. Besides, I wasn't afraid of Jana. Her words hadn't hurt me, and I was entirely unbothered by her attitude. She'd caught me off guard with the honey water, but beyond that, she was no match for me. "I see your remorse was greatly exaggerated."

"Just because I don't like you doesn't mean I want you dead. I didn't know you were allergic, and I wasn't trying to kill you."

"No, you were trying to humiliate me."

She shrugged one shoulder and lifted an eyebrow.

"I don't know what you think I did to you, but—"

"You tried to steal my boyfriend," she snapped.

"No, I didn't."

"Yes, you did." She glared. "You were always flaunting yourself in front of him to get his attention. He couldn't keep his eyes off you whenever you walked into a room. He even stopped touching—"

"That's enough," Axel snapped, spinning her around to look at him.

"Fuck you." She ripped her arm out of his grasp and faced me again. "See, he's doing it again. Choosing you."

"He's not." I shook my head and told her the honest to goddess truth. "From the moment I met him, he wanted nothing to do with me. I was never your competition. You're the one he chose, and he made that clear on more than one occasion. Whatever problems you have with him have nothing to do with me, and they never will." I spoke directly to her, but I didn't miss when Axel closed his eyes and bowed his head at my words. With each sentence, his shoulders slumped and his chest deflated. "I promise you, Jana—Axel never wanted me."

She didn't say anything, and I took her silence as an opportunity to leave. We were nearly through the exit when she yelled, "Are you going to accept my apology?"

Stopping, I turned to look at her. "When you offer me a sincere apology, I'll accept. Until then, no."

Vale and I were outside the school entrance gates when we heard them arguing behind us, but we ignored it and carried on with our lives. We enjoyed a romantic dinner together before returning to Araphel, where we spent our first night in our mated dorm happily wrapped around each other.

Chapter Twelve

"Maybe she's in love with him?" Brev said around a mouthful of salsa. "Why else would she be so jealous over someone who's not her mate?"

Vale and I had invited all my friends, Puck, and Roko, over for takeout and drinks so they could see the dorm once we'd settled in. It had been a couple of days, and we were excited to have them over. Even though it was temporary, it felt like home.

The mated dorms were unique living spaces, fully customized to cater to the needs and desires of each mated group. The building was located away from the single dorms, and the residence hall was spacious, with room for growth inside and out. Each mated suite was equipped with everything single rooms had, including a kitchen, living space, and a bathroom. However, instead of one bedroom, they had two, and more could be added as needed. Mated groups weren't expected to share a single bed or room, and having private space was crucial to a bond's overall well-being. The building sat along the forest's edge, so any changes made didn't affect the other parts of the academy. It made perfect sense, considering each bond group was unique and required different things to be happy and content. After graduation, the room would be reset for new tenants.

Our top-floor room had been customized to include a large balcony and floor-to-ceiling glass doors that let in plenty of sunshine. The balcony was spacious enough to accommodate Vale's shifted form, and the doors were wide enough for him to rest his dragon head inside the living room if he wanted to. Having a place with ample space to shift was crucial to Vale so he could take flight without worrying about who was around. The architect had made the same adjustments to our room that Vale had had at High Crest, and though the view wasn't the same, he was happy with the modifications.

The living room was comfortable and cozy, with a huge sectional sofa, oversized recliner chairs, and a roaring fireplace. We sat around with our friends as Vale and I recounted our unfortunate run-in with Axel and Jana. We'd dished up plates of pizza, chips, salsa, and pretzels with beer cheese when the topic came up.

"If that's true, I feel a little sorry for her." I didn't want to pity my bully, but it made sense why she hated me so much.

"She doesn't deserve your sympathy," Puck grumbled. "Yeah, it sucks for her if she's in love with such an asshole, but it doesn't excuse her shitty attitude and actions, Lyra."

"I'm not saying that it's justified. But if it's true, and he—"

"Was obsessed with you."

"Always stared at you in front of her."

"Watched your every move instead of paying attention to her."

"Didn't feel the same," I said, speaking over my friends. "If she expressed her feelings, and he didn't reciprocate them, I can understand how hurt she would be."

Vale leaned over and kissed my head. "She still doesn't deserve your kindness."

"Maybe not." I shrugged. "But I can't help it. Being rejected by a fated mate changed me. It made me question everything I thought I knew about love and destiny. And in the aftermath, I found myself on the receiving end of negativity and animosity I'd never experienced before. I was put in situations and circumstances that I probably wouldn't have encountered otherwise, and as a result, I realize now more than ever the importance of kindness, empathy, and understanding toward others. I see things differently now. It was as if the ground itself shifted and threw me off balance. I had to learn how to walk again in a suddenly unfamiliar and unpredictable world. As painful as it was, the experience forced me to confront my own assumptions and beliefs. Maybe this was my lesson. Regardless, for that reason, I can't help but be sympathetic because if what you're saying is true, Jana and I share the same pain."

Callie took my hand, but everyone stayed quiet except for my brother.

"I love you, baby sister, and you're going to be a thoughtful Queen one day, but she's a bitch, and I don't feel sorry for her. If she fell for someone who wasn't her fated mate and got mad when the feelings weren't returned, she's not only a bitch—she's stupid too."

My mouth fell open. "Puck, that's not nice!"

"Sorry, not sorry." He raised his brows. "I don't like her. I never liked her, and after what she did to you, she can rot for all I care."

Sidric lifted his beer to Puck. "Agreed."

Jed, Brev, and Roko did the same.

Vale nodded in agreement, but Callie surprised me the most when she leaned forward and tapped Puck's beer with her own. "Here, here."

"You guys..."

Vale put his hand on my back and rubbed small circles as he said, "It's not that we don't agree with how you feel about the situation. We support you, but we also have feelings about what happened, and the two aren't mutually exclusive. You may be sympathetic, but I'm not, and I will never forgive her—or Axel. Whatever her problem is, she needs to leave you out of it and figure it out for herself. If she ever says or does anything to you again, I will not stand by and let her get away with it. And she better not piss me off enough that I shift because my baser instincts are harder to control with logic in animal form."

My belly flipped at his protectiveness, and if our friends weren't there, I would have launched myself at him and kissed his stern, sexy face.

"So now that we all agree Lyra is a marshmallow and Jana can fuck off for life, what do you think they were arguing about?" Roko asked. He took a massive bite of pizza and spoke around the saucy, cheesy dough. “She said their parents wanted them to go somewhere together. Where and for what?”

Vale leaned back and crossed one leg over the other. “The Winter Mating Revelry.”

Callie wrinkled her nose. “Why?”

“Their parents have been sending them to mating balls together for the last couple of years.” Vale shrugged.

“But she wasn’t at the Spring Court Revelry.” I looked at him. “If she had been, she would know what happened.”

“That’s true,” Puck agreed. “She’s so far up his ass that she would definitely know.”

“And we’re still sure she doesn’t?” Roko asked. “I know we talked about this before, but it would make sense that she knew, based on her behavior.”

Puck shook his head. “It would fit the narrative, but no. She wasn’t there. We knew the guest list before going and double-checked it afterward. It’s protocol. Even though Lyra’s geas is typically foolproof, we always know who’s at these events and keep tabs on them after for security reasons.”

Brev wrinkled his brow. “Why?”

“If anything comes up as far as rumors are concerned, we can look into them.”

“Since guests would be the most likely to speculate,” Vale added.

“Correct.” Puck sat back and took a swig of his beer. “For instance, with the Spring Revelry, rumors about a cover-up spread through the Spring Court staff because no one had ever seen or worked with someone who looked like Lyra. They weren’t wrong, but we couldn’t let the gossip continue. So our brother, Shea, cast an illusion over Tunder, Cleon, and me that looks similar to Lyra’s geas form. The four of us took turns going to the Spring Court. We were seen dusting a room or entering and exiting a space for staff only. We leaked a name and position, and then, after a couple of weeks, we put a transfer in for a new job.”

“And that worked?”

Puck smirked. “Yeah. People will believe anything under the right circumstances.”

Brev squinted his eyes at my brother. "How many times have you tricked us?"

"None." Puck rolled his eyes. "Why would I waste my time when you know everything?"

"So Jana definitely wasn't at the Spring Revelry then, otherwise everyone would know what happened." Callie sipped her drink.

"Not necessarily." Puck shook his head. "Jana could have posed a problem if she had been present, and the staff started spreading rumors based on the cover story that was used. But the guest list included females who resembled Lyra's geas. Adding to that, with the ball theme and color scheme, it's possible that any one of them could have been the person Axel was seen talking to."

"Plausible deniability." Roko's eyes lit up.

"Exactly." Puck winked at him.

"Plus, the geas itself is enchanted with an illusory charm before events. It serves to dissuade anyone from paying too much attention to me, except for my potential mates," I told them.

"That's why Landor didn't know who you were when you came to Araphel. Even though he was there that night." Jed grinned with realization.

"Precisely."

"Every time I hang out with you, I learn so much about court politics," Sidric said, chuckling. "What a crazy life you live."

"Anyway, I don't know why Jana wasn't at the Spring ball," Vale said. "But I know they've attended every other one together. It's only a guess that she was referencing the revelry, but since it's only a few weeks away, I'd bet that's what they were arguing about."

"So what does that mean for Lyra? If you're all there, will you connect with Axel again?" Callie's eyes widened as she pieced it all together.

"I don't know," I told her quietly.

Vale put his arm around me. "That's the concern. Her parents are consulting the High Priestess, and they'll let us know what they've decided."

Puck dipped a chip in salsa. "Either they'll have to pull strings and keep Axel away, or Lyra will have to skip another ceremony. Finding her other mates is more important, but Axel and his family might become a problem when they're told they can't attend."

"Or worse—they could start questioning why," Sidric added.

"Exactly."

"What a shit show." Brev leaned back in his chair and kicked one leg over the other. "No offense, Lyra, but I'm glad I'm not one of your mates. This cloak-and-dagger shit is way above my pay grade."

Jed smacked him. "You're an idiot."

"Ow." Brev rubbed his arm. "I'm not insulting anyone! I just want to play Starball, fuck, find my mate, fuck a lot more, and start a business. Simple. That's all I meant."

Vale and I both chuckled.

"I don't take any offense," I said. "This life isn't for everyone."

"I'm also glad you're not one of her mates," Vale grumbled. "I like you well enough as a friend, but the thought of you with my Lyra makes me want to burn you to a crisp. No offense."

Brev snorted, patting Sidric on the shoulder. "Sucks to be you, pal."

Sidric shook his head while we laughed, but Vale gave him a pass. "Sidric's cool. He was there for Lyra during a difficult time. Besides, he'll be in my shoes someday. He'll have to pay it forward."

"Threats from a lynx shifter don't hit the same, dragon." Sidric smirked.

Vale barked out a laugh. Then they bantered about swiftness versus size, which led to stamina, and before it went totally off the rails, I held up a hand.

"As much fun as it is to listen to you two, there is a point to this story." I scooted next to Callie. "We want you all to attend the Winter Revelry with us."

That shut everyone up.

"Why?" Jed whined. "The court revelries are so stuffy and formal. They're boring. Can't we do the town festival instead?"

"Yeah, I don't even own a tuxedo." Brev shook his head.

"Liar." Puck threw his napkin at him. "You wore one to the championship dinner a few weeks ago, you dingus."

"Fine. I don't like the taste of wine, and the festivals have beer," he countered.

As the males argued, I turned to Callie. “It’ll be fun. We can go dress shopping.”

“Oh, you don’t have to convince me!” Callie beamed. “I’ve only been to one formal revelry, and I’m always down for shopping and buying new clothes.”

Chapter Thirteen

Vale

"What is this movie called again?" Lyra's sweet breath warmed my chest as she spoke. When our friends left, I'd convinced her to watch a movie with me on the sofa—after I'd given her several orgasms, of course.

We were working our way through the entire space, and though I wasn't jealous of Lyra and Sidric's past, I was unabashedly possessive of her. So as soon as they were gone, I'd pleasured her in the chair he'd used.

I'd bent her over the back, spreading her wide as I had her for dessert, and before she'd fully come down from her first orgasm, I'd plunged into her heat and given her another. Then I'd flipped her around and slid her down my cock so she could ride me. She came for me twice before I'd shamelessly filled her up with my release. She was so drained that I had to hold her against me as she'd shuddered through her fourth orgasm, and afterwards, I'd carried her to the bathroom to get cleaned up.

She nearly fell asleep in the bath as I'd washed her hair. But as we'd toweled off, she became hungry again, compelling me to provide her with sustenance. And that's how I'd persuaded her to come and sit with me on the couch.

It was early enough that neither of us wanted to go to bed, but breaking in the furniture had worn her out, so this was a great compromise.

"It's called *Eòin Fuse*."

"And he's mad because someone took his cat?" she asked through a yawn.

Her attempt to stay awake for my benefit was so adorable I couldn't help but chuckle. "The mob killed his cat to send him a message, so now he's hunting them down."

"Good for him." She yawned again, and I pulled her closer. "It's rude to kill someone's pet," she mumbled as she buried her face in my neck.

Her breathing evened out, and her body relaxed as she fell asleep in my arms—which was absolutely the most amazing feeling. Her trust and acceptance made me feel more powerful than when I was in dragon form. I wanted to cherish this time together because I knew it wouldn't be the two of us forever. I wasn't upset about that, but being her first mate was a gift. I had her all to myself for the time being, and it was more than I ever could have imagined.

Finding your mate was a dream come true, but everyone I knew fantasized about being the first. Unless you were one of the rare ones to only have one mate, you knew you were destined to share with others, and while it was expected and wonderful, I was going to enjoy every damn minute of our time alone.

I wasn't paying attention to the movie as I watched her sleep in my arms. When a shadowy figure appeared on the balcony, I was as angry as I was smug. He hadn't caught me off guard; I was simply annoyed that he'd had the audacity to show up on our doorstep as if he had any right to be there. Despite his posturing, I'd been watching him since I arrived, and Lyra's friends were right—Axel couldn't keep his eyes off my mate.

I didn't feel sorry for him, and I would never forgive him, but I knew Axel. He was still the Axel I'd always known, and I was sure he was kicking himself as he watched me with Lyra. A part of him hated that I was experiencing these firsts instead of him.

Sucks to suck.

I didn't want him looking at her, though, especially while she was so vulnerable. As much as I wanted to show off, the thought of using her to make him envious made me sick.

I carefully lifted her from the couch, shielding her from his view as I took her to bed and tucked her in. When she was snuggled in the blankets, I kissed her perfect lips and whispered that I'd join her soon. She gave me a dreamy smile and mumbled something before falling back asleep.

I clicked off the light and shut the door, storming outside to confront my uninvited guest.

"What are you doing here?" I growled, fighting the urge to shift. As a dragon, I was naturally aggressive, and I worked hard to keep that part of myself in check. But being around the person I' thought was as important to me as my mate, while knowing everything he'd done and said to hurt her, made it difficult not to squash him under my foot.

"She looks so tiny in your arms," he whispered, staring at the door to our bedroom.

"Don't talk about her." I stepped forward, cutting off his view. He couldn't see Lyra, but I didn't like him imagining her asleep in bed. "Answer my question."

"You said we could talk."

"That wasn't an invitation for you to be a fucking creeper outside my home and watch me through the window with my mate."

"She's my..." The words stuck in his throat. He shook his head and stepped back. "I wasn't thinking."

"You're lucky she's such a gentle soul, Axel, or I wouldn't be having this conversation with you."

"I know I broke this," he said, waving his hand between us. He included the dorm in the sweeping gesture as if to include Lyra.

Pretending I was okay with his presence was testing my patience, and I wasn't sure I could hold it for long without exploding.

"Look." I crossed my arms over my chest to hide my fists that wanted to punch in his face again. "Things will never be the same between us."

His face went slack. "I know."

"But after talking with my mate and taking a few days to cool off..." I was at a loss for words. I wanted nothing to do with him. I didn't want to try, and I certainly didn't want to make amends. I finally decided to lean into the truth. "We've known each other our whole lives."

"You're my best friend, Vale."

I gave him one quick nod, and his shoulders relaxed as if we had agreed to something. In a way, I suppose we had. I led him to the water, and he drank it. I hoped he'd choke.

"We need ground rules," I grumbled. "First and foremost, Lyra is off-limits."

He drew back, almost looking annoyed. "What do you mean?"

"You stay away from her."

"I'm not going to hurt her."

"This isn't a negotiation, Axel. The topic of my mate is off limits," I growled. It was the most honest thing I'd said so far. "Don't talk about her, don't ask about her, and don't fucking spy on her."

He ground his teeth and looked away. "What else?"

"I don't know yet, but if you don't agree, we're done here."

"I shouldn't have been watching you," he said, glaring. "I'm sorry."

"What exactly are you sorry for, Axel?" I scowled.

"More than I can put into words," he mumbled, gazing into the living room.

"If you want to talk, you have my number. And you could have knocked on the door."

He nodded, but he didn't look at me. He just kept staring at the dorm. "You're right. I wanted to see ... you."

I couldn't help it. I snorted. It wasn't funny, but he was so obvious. The longing on his face matched everything I'd seen and heard. "Sure. You wanted to see *me*. Right."

He glared at me again, but it lacked heat. He was self-conscious about being called on his lie. I'd been reading the emotions on his face since we were kids.

"Are you regretting your choice, *brother*?" I sneered. I had to ask—none of this made sense, and I needed to understand.

"Don't."

"Don't what, Axel?"

"Don't make me lie to you."

I stepped so close that our noses nearly touched. "What the fuck does that mean?"

Instead of getting mad like I'd expected, he closed his eyes and leaned forward, practically shoving his face in my neck where Lyra had been only a few moments ago.

"You smell like her," he whispered, and the desperation in his voice set my teeth on edge.

I shoved him away, and he nearly fell on his ass as he tripped over his feet.

"What the hell is wrong with you?" I tried to stay quiet so I didn't wake Lyra, but between my yelling and Axel's stumbling, I wasn't hopeful.

Axel shook his head and glanced at the bedroom with panicked eyes when a light came on. "I'm sorry."

"I told you she was off-limits."

"I know." He raised his hands. "I know. I'll do better."

"Leave. Now. Before she sees you. You have no idea what you've done, and she deserves to feel safe in her home. Don't come back here, Axel."

He didn't respond but stepped back.

"And don't call me; I'll call you," I added before he turned away. I needed him to leave believing we were still friends—with boundaries, of course.

"Thank you. Take care of her," he said as he summoned a vine from a nearby tree and disappeared from view.

I spun around and opened the door, stepping inside as a sleepy Lyra wandered down the hall.

Her voice was low and a little scratchy as she asked, "Is everything okay?"

After locking the door and closing the blinds, I swept her up in my arms and turned off the lights. "Yes, my mate, everything is fine. Let's go back to bed."

Chapter Fourteen

"And you're sure you're okay with it?" Callie asked.

After a lot of back and forth, my family had finally agreed that we should tell our friends about the plan regarding Axel. They obviously couldn't know everything since it was Night Court business and a matter of realm security, but they needed to know something since Vale would have to fake a friendship with Axel.

Telling them nothing would prompt questions, and after everything we'd been through over the last several months, they would be suspicious if not concerned. I also wasn't comfortable lying to them about something so important.

We'd told them what they needed to know about the new threat and suspicions of Axel's involvement, but nothing more. It was enough, and they'd understood that the less they knew, the better.

I had cast a privacy spell around us so Callie and I could speak freely in Earth Rejuvenation class. It was the first real alone time we'd had since I met Vale, and after filling her in on everything I'd been up to with my mate, we discussed Axel.

"I am okay with it because I know he's doing this for us." I stretched out on the grass and let the sun warm my face as my body absorbed the earth's magic.

"I think it will be more difficult for Vale. I'm not the one that has to spend time with him while pretending everything is normal."

She snorted. "I'll be surprised if it lasts."

I sat up and looked at her, but her eyes were closed as she snickered at her joke. "Why do you say that?"

She turned her head, wrinkling her brow. "Dude, he totally hates Axel. Do you really think Vale can be Axel's fake buddy without breaking his face?"

"Yes."

Her smile grew, and she sat up to face me. "Let's bet."

"What?"

"Come on. Let's make a friendly little wager." She wiggled her brows.

I smirked, seeing how eager she was. She had that look in her eye—the same focused excitement she'd gotten when she wanted to work on my honey allergy.

"I give him one week," Callie said.

"You think he'll fail in a week?" My eyes widened. "That's not very—"

"Not fail," she interrupted, shaking her head. "I just think he'll make him a knuckle sandwich. I don't know him, but he doesn't strike me as the type to give up. He does have a temper, though, and we've all seen it."

"You're not wrong." I blushed, knowing his temper was tied to his need to protect me. I wondered if I'd ever get used to the feeling or if I'd always be weak in the knees for my mate. "I don't feel comfortable betting on my mate, though. It feels back-stabby." I shook my head. "I don't want to."

"Oh, fine." Callie's shoulders dropped. "But I still think I'm right."

"I don't." I stood and dusted off my skirt, reaching my hand out to help her up. "But out of curiosity, what would you have bet?"

"I don't know." She shrugged. "Maybe you could pick my gown for the ball if I lost, and you'd have to tell me how big Vale's dragon dick is if I won."

My mouth fell open. "Callie!"

She rolled her eyes and linked our arms together. "Oh, hush. I know you're not a prude. You told me about Sidric."

"I did not."

"Fine. But you told me he was good. That's basically the same thing. Why won't you tell me about Vale?" She sucked in a breath and turned to me. "Oh, unless... He's bad, isn't he?"

"What?"

"He's a bad lay, and you're embarrassed. Oh, my sweet friend, I'm so sorry."

"I'm not falling for this." I shook my head and started walking. "You're trying to trick me, and it won't work."

"You know, sometimes it's annoying having a smart friend who can figure me out so quickly."

I chuckled. "You love it."

She rested her head on my shoulder. "I do."

I dropped the privacy spell once we joined the other students. It was rude to keep it up just for the sake of it, and I was more than happy to move on to a different topic.

"So, shopping this weekend? There's this cute little boutique I thought we could go to."

"That sounds fun." She beamed. "I'm surprised you don't have a curator, though."

"In a way, I do, but I've never had a friend to go dress shopping with before."

"Aw." She gave me a pouty smile. "That's sweet and sort of sad, Lyra. We'll make a whole day of it. We'll have brunch with mimosas, and shopping and pedicures."

"Yes, please!"

"It's a date." She smirked. "Don't tell your mate, or he'll want to break *my* face too."

"I wouldn't dream of it." Vale stuck his head between us, and I squealed in surprise. Another squeak fell from my lips when he lifted me and flipped me over his shoulder. "As long as it's a platonic date and you're only doing toes and dresses."

"And food," Callie added helpfully while I squirmed to cover my ass.

"Vale." I pinched his side, but he didn't put me down. He just placed his hand over the bottom of my skirt so I didn't flash my panties to the quad.

He kissed my thigh and slid me down his front, pecking my lips with a grin. "Hi."

"Hi." I smiled against his mouth, wrapping my legs around his waist. "I thought you were busy this afternoon."

"I am, but I wanted to see you first." He squeezed my ass. "Will you be home when I'm done? I ... might be in a mood."

It sounded like he was hinting at sex, but since he was going to talk to Axel, I knew the mood he was referring to wasn't the fun kind.

"I'll be home. I have assignments to work on. What are you doing for dinner?"

"I don't know yet." He sighed.

"I'll have something waiting for you, just in case." I kissed him once more, then hopped down. "Callie and I were going to get something at the dining hall, anyway."

"Thanks." He pressed his lips to the top of my head. "I'll see you later. Bye, Callie."

She looked up from her phone long enough to nod. "Later, dude."

I gave Vale an encouraging smile as he left.

"He doesn't seem very excited."

I shook my head. "He's not."

"So, what colors are we wearing?" Callie stuffed her phone in her back pocket. "It's the Winter Revelry, and with the theme, I'm thinking silver or blue."

As we walked toward the dining hall, discussing our plans for our shopping day, a strange sensation crawled up the base of my neck. I looked around, but nothing seemed out of the ordinary. It felt like I was being watched. The tingling reminded me of Shea's magic when he projected illusions.

Then, as we reached the door, it was gone.

"Did you feel that?"

She wrinkled her brow. "Feel what?"

"I'm not sure." I studied the room. "I thought I felt something."

Callie put her hand on my arm. "Are you okay?"

"Yeah. I swear, it felt like someone was behind us."

She shook her head. "I didn't see anyone."

"It's probably just my imagination."

"Or a little anxiety about where your mate is?" She raised a brow at me and pulled me through the door. "It's perfectly normal to feel worried. If I could shift into a fly, I'd be on the wall listening to that conversation. I'd pay money to hear Axel's justifications for what he did."

I snorted. "You're probably right. I know Vale's fine. It's still awkward, though."

"That's an understatement, but sure, let's go with awkward."

After getting some food, we sat at our usual table. I tried to focus on our conversation, but that strange feeling lingered in the back of my mind. I couldn't seem to shake it off. When we finished our dinner, I grabbed something for Vale before saying goodnight to Callie since I couldn't concentrate.

I was relieved to return to my dorm, and after I put on comfy clothes, I flopped down on the couch to wait for Vale. I didn't think the weird feeling was anything serious, but to be safe, I texted my brothers, planning to tell Vale when he came back.

Luckily, they didn't get worked up about it and agreed that it was probably a symptom of stress or anxiety. Hopefully, Vale would agree without going all alpha-male-possessive-boyfriend on me.

Chapter Fifteen

I was so distracted walking into my Earth Elemental class the next day that I didn't realize the room had been rearranged until I went to take my seat.

I looked up from the book I was reading for Political Science, scanning the class and noticing I wasn't alone in my confusion. I didn't like being surprised, especially in a setting like this.

"Please check the new seating arrangement," Professor Rootsworth announced. She didn't look up from her desk as she pointed to the board behind her, where each student's name was listed with a table number next to it.

My name was at the top of the list, so I quickly found my spot. The tables were spread out more than the original seating, and I was now at the back corner table.

Since it was a second-year class and everyone already knew the basic principles of their elemental magic, we'd been studying the unique properties and characteristics of our elements, such as earth's solidity and stability. We also discussed advanced techniques for manipulation and refining our control.

Partner exercises played a central role in the class. Working closely with each other to develop our abilities was important because it allowed us to share knowledge, insight, and experience with our partners. Some of us had a natural affinity for controlling plant growth while others had an easier time manipulating stone and earth.

I'd pulled my things out of my bag when I saw Axel from my peripheral.

After the honey incident, he'd kept his distance and stayed out of my sight, so I nearly forgot he was in class with me.

I was too stunned to say anything as he approached the table, so instead, we awkwardly stared at each other until he finally broke the silence.

"I don't want you to be uncomfortable." He adjusted his bag and took a step back. "I'll go talk to her about switching partners."

The immediate disappointment I felt had me reaching out and putting my hand on his forearm before I realized what I was doing.

"No. It's fine," I said, but he wasn't listening.

His eyes were focused on where my hand rested on his arm. I shouldn't have felt comfortable touching him, but some instinct left behind from our broken bond had led me to the action without my conscious consent.

His skin was warm, and the hair was soft despite the muscle being hard against my palm. His earthy musk filled my nose, reminding me of Vale's smoke and fire scent, which always grew stronger when he was feeling a *certain* way about me.

Axel breathed deeply, and the movement of his chest drew my eyes. Time slowed as I took him in, and the air warmed around us. He was so tall it felt like I trailed my eyes up every inch of his chest and neck before I focused on his lips. He parted them and pulled in a shaky breath. At the sound, my eyes snapped up to his. He was staring at me so intently that I felt exposed.

When he stepped forward again, I snapped out of it, jerking my hand from his arm and pulling it against myself.

The tension shattered in an instant, and in its place was the painful disappointment I'd felt moments ago. "Forgive me. I shouldn't have—"

"I'm sorry," he interrupted, lifting his hand as if to reach out to me, but he stopped it mid-air, lingering like he was unsure what to do. "I'm… I'll go ask Ms. Rootsworth to reassign me." He shoved his hands in his pockets and turned.

We had been in our own bubble for so long that the other students were already settled, chatting and comparing notes.

I decided I wouldn't disrupt class because of our issues. I told myself it was a lesson in diplomatic relations. I'd probably have to spend time with people I didn't like in the future. Just because you were a figurehead didn't mean you got along with everyone you were required to work with. My situation wasn't any different.

"Axel, wait," I said, and he stopped instantly. "We can make this work."

He spun around so quickly that my hair lifted, tickling my nose. His eyes went wide, and I swear I felt the temperature rising as he stared at me with an emotion I couldn't place.

"Lyra?" he asked, his voice sounding confused but optimistic.

I didn't know why he'd be hopeful, but I couldn't allow myself to wonder either. Nothing good had ever come from my interactions with him, and though I was willing to do this, I wouldn't spend any time trying to figure him out.

"You don't need a new assignment. We can put our differences aside and work together for this hour."

It took him a second to respond, but when he did, he sighed heavily enough that his shoulders dropped. "Right. Of course that's what you meant," he said quietly.

"Unless this is a problem for you?" I fidgeted with the pen in my hand. "I don't want to—"

"No." He stepped closer. "No. It's not a problem for me. As long as you're sure."

"It's fine, Axel. I know you don't like me, but we don't have to be friends to work together." I gave him a small smile and turned away. It was too hard to speak to him like this, like we were two normal people in a class together.

He moved with intention as he set his bag down and pulled out his chair, almost as if he didn't want to startle me.

"You don't need to tiptoe around me," I muttered.

He nodded, grabbing his things from his bag with less finesse. Then he slouched down in his chair and drummed his fingers on his notebook while we waited for Ms. Rootsworth to start class.

"Thank you for letting Vale and me stay friends."

I shook my head at the ridiculous statement but tried to keep my tone friendly as I replied, "Vale is a grown man who can make his own decisions. I have nothing but respect for him. If he wants to be friends with you, that's his choice. He doesn't require my permission for anything, and I won't control whom he can and can't speak to, Axel. That's not how a mate bond works."

Crossing his arms over his chest, he kept his eyes on my face before turning to stare at the front of the class.

"I wouldn't know," he muttered.

"No, you wouldn't," I said.

His lips pinched together as he closed his eyes, but he didn't respond. The longer we sat together in silence, the more the air filled with tension around us. Distracting myself, I scanned through my notes so I knew exactly what I was in for with this partnership.

Some assignments would be more challenging than others, especially the ones where we were required to share our power through touch. A strange, nervous anticipation fluttered in my belly at the thought. My palms started to sweat, and my finger stuck to the page when I turned it.

Axel's voice made me jump when he asked, "Are you sure you're alright with this?"

My brow wrinkled at the odd question, and when I looked at him, he seemed genuinely concerned. "Yes, why?"

He dipped his head, and I realized my leg was bouncing up and down like my bones were trying to jump out of my skin.

I looked back at my notes. "You have to admit this is a little awkward. I'll try not to disturb you."

"You're not disturbing me," he said, sitting up and leaning forward to look at me. "And I don't want you to think I don't like—"

"Alright, class," Professor Rootsworth called. "Now that you've gotten acquainted with your partners, let's get started. You've been paired together for specific reasons, so if you are thinking of asking for a change, save your breath—the answer is no. Now, for your first assignment..."

Professor Rootsworth dove into her lecture, so whatever Axel was going to say, he never got the chance. She outlined the next several weeks and what we would do together. The more she spoke, the more nervous I became. Axel and I would have to spend a lot of time together.

I was anxious about the classwork, but I was more worried about how Vale would take the news. He'd been adamant that Axel kept his distance, and now it seemed like I would be spending more time with Axel than even Vale was.

As if he could read my mind, Axel cleared his throat as she finished informing us of her expectations.

"Vale will understand," he whispered.

The sound of my mate's name coming from his mouth made me turn. When I did, I found we were only inches apart, and his words and proximity froze me in place.

"I promise I will not make this difficult for you. I know you have no reason to believe me or trust me, but I won't do anything to hurt you. Never again," he added quietly.

"Okay." My voice was lower than his, barely more than a whisper, and when his eyes flicked to my lips, my breathing sped up.

"I will be on my best behavior," he said, keeping his eyes locked on my lips. "And we will keep this professional ... if that's what you want."

"Mr. Stonebrook, please see me after class," Professor Rootsworth interrupted ... whatever was happening between us.

Axel stared at me for a few more seconds before looking away.

"Yes, ma'am." He smirked at her, but I knew the humor in his eyes wasn't for the professor or her request.

I just wasn't sure why it was for me and what it meant.

Chapter Sixteen

"If we explain to the administration, they'll let you drop the class," Vale grumbled for the third time.

He wasn't just upset that Axel and I were in the same classes or that we were partnered together—he was upset I wouldn't pull strings to get out of the situation.

"I was supposed to be dealing with him, not you. I don't like it," he argued as he paced around the living room.

"You're going to wear a hole in the carpet, which is brand new."

"I'll rearrange my schedule tomorrow and go with you," he announced as he pulled out his phone.

Before I could respond, someone knocked.

Vale opened the door to Puck, and my brother held up his hand. "Let me in before you pick up where you left off when you were berating me on the phone."

Dumbfounded, I stood from the couch and watched as all four of my brothers entered our dorm.

Puck and Roko led the way, wearing their faces, but my other brothers wore illusions cast by Shea. They'd been using the same ones for years. It was how we could be in public together without drawing suspicion. Once they were inside and a privacy spell had been put up, Shea dropped the illusion so we could see them properly.

"You called my brothers?"

"Of course I did." Vale crossed his arms over his chest. "What good is it being a Knight if I can't pull strings to keep the Night Princess safe?"

I walked around the couch and stood in front of him. "This is different."

"It isn't. This is about your safety."

I shook my head and put my hands on his arms. "I'm not in danger."

"You're not wrong, but Vale was right to call us." Shea wandered through the living room as he spoke. "I don't think you're in danger from a class assignment, but because it's Axel, we needed to know."

Vale scowled at Shea. "He was the reason she was attacked. She almost died because of him. How is she not in danger?"

"You're thinking irrationally." Puck cracked open a sparkling water he'd stolen from the kitchen.

Vale turned his glare to Puck. "Why aren't you thinking irrationally?"

"Because my mate has been talking me down for the last twenty minutes while I waited for these three to show up." Puck flopped on the couch and kicked his feet onto the table. "I've had the benefit of a cool-down time."

"Well, lucky fucking you," Vale grumbled, pulling me into his chest. "Enlighten me then."

"You're not overreacting," Tunder said. He stood in front of the little fireplace with his hands in his pockets. His presence was always calming. He looked cuddly in his sweater vest and corduroy jeans but not stuffy and aged like my accounting instructor, Professor Reginald Copperplate. No, Tunder's broad chest, muscular arms, trim waist, and perfectly coiffed hair were anything but frumpy. "You are reacting as a Fae who wants to protect his mate, which is perfectly understandable. However, we all knew that Lyra had classes with Axel and this was a possibility."

"We have to tread carefully on how we react to their proximity," Cleon explained. "We've had this discussion several times—once when we found out that Axel was in attendance, and again when we realized she would be in several of his classes."

"And another after the honey attack," Shea added, resting against the counter and kicking one ankle over the other. "We all wanted him removed then, but we had to step back and look at it as if she's not the future Queen."

"Believe me, Vale. We've been where you are. True, you're her mate and it is different, but as her brothers, we feel protective of her too," Tunder said.

"So, while we didn't know how close they'd have to work together, it was a reality we prepared for," Cleon shrugged.

"Well, most of us, anyway." Shea leaned forward and smacked Puck on the head. "Don't let this idiot's casual demeanor fool you. He was in an uproar when he called, and wanted the entire Night Guard put on duty."

"Puck." I shook my head.

"I just forgot about the plan," Puck said, rolling his eyes.

Roko chuckled. "Yeah, because you jump to conclusions."

"If there's a plan, I should have been told," Vale said.

I raised my brows at my brothers. "You should have told both of us. Why weren't we informed, and what *is* the plan?"

Tunder walked over and put his hands on my shoulders. "We didn't inform you because we hoped you'd never have to deal with this. We didn't want to give you something to stress about in case it never happened. You should be enjoying your time here, Lala. You've been pushed into this responsibility too early." He kissed the top of my head and moved back to stand by the fireplace. "Plus, we are doing as our parents instructed."

"And the plan is simple. It's nothing, honestly." Shea shook his head. "There isn't a lot we can do to intervene, so you're not getting out of the assignment with Axel. We have been able to control the location for your gem hunt assignment, though."

"The crystal cave Professor Rootsworth normally uses wasn't available this time," Cleon winked.

I snorted. "You guys are ridiculous."

"Not even a little, baby sister." Puck gave me a toothy smile.

"The other location is farther from school but closer to the Night Guard training facility, and they happen to be doing tactical drills on the same day the gem hunt was approved," Shea said, nodding at Vale.

I looked up at Vale with a grin. "See, nothing to worry about."

He didn't return my enthusiasm. He kissed my temple but continued to glare at my brothers. "I want to know everything. Plans, protection, anything you've got up your sleeves for instances like this, and anything I haven't even considered yet."

Tunder glanced at my other brothers before saying, "We discussed that on the way over. We were inclined to let you know as things arose, so you two could enjoy your time here." He gave Vale a smirk. "But you seem to share Puck's penchant for leaping before you look. So we will brief you on everything. It's your right to know, and I think it'll be easier for everyone if you do."

Shea, Cleon, and Roko all chuckled. Puck rolled his eyes and told them to fuck off before kissing his mate. "Not you, babe. Just those three jackasses."

"One last thing." Shea pushed off the counter and came to stand in front of me. Reaching into his pocket, he pulled out a necklace and held it for me to inspect.

"What's this?" I touched the gemstone and spun it around. It was a clear crystal pendant cradled with silver spirals and leaves on a delicate chain.

"Father imbued it with intangibility," Shea announced, and I felt my brows try to disappear into my hairline.

Father's intangibility gift was rare, but that he could cast it into a vessel for someone else to use was even more unique. His Divination was in Affliction, and the ability allowed him to pass through anything solid—literally anything. The only downside to him sharing his gift was the time limit for the user. He didn't have that to contend with, though.

"How long?" I took the necklace and marveled at the gift. He'd only ever given it to my mother and fathers before.

"Thirty minutes." Shea took it back and unclasped the lock.

Vale loosened his hold and gave me space so I could turn, and Shea promptly fastened the necklace around my neck.

"Thirty minutes will be plenty of time for you to get somewhere safe." Cleon came over and lifted the gem that rested on my breastbone. "We know you're powerful. You could shift if you needed to."

"But that would expose me."

"Correct." He booped my nose. "But sometimes running away is the safest choice. Especially when you can go through walls."

"This is only a precaution, Lyra. I truly don't believe you're in danger from Axel," Tunder said, raising his hands when Puck and Vale sat up to argue. "I know you both have strong feelings about this. I understand. Yes, what happened to Lyra is directly linked to Axel, but he isn't the one who hurt her."

"Physically," Vale sneered.

Tunder nodded.

"I'm not in danger," I said, and everyone focused on me. "My unease around Axel isn't because I'm scared for my safety. I just don't want to get my feelings hurt."

"That's more than enough reason to stay away." Vale's hot breath spilled down my neck. I wasn't sure if his breath was just that warm or if he was holding back his dragon.

"But he hasn't said or done anything since the attack, right?" Tunder prodded.

I shook my head. "He hasn't said anything mean or threatening—nothing like that."

Tunder smiled at me and then at the others in the room. "Which is how I know she's protected. We don't have to like it or like her spending time with him, but she is safe from him."

"How are you so sure about this?" Puck asked.

"The sibling pact you all seem to have forgotten about, that's how."

Shea chuckled. "That's right. Even if Lyra didn't want to admit to something, she couldn't help it because the deal we made wouldn't allow it."

Cleon clapped Tunder on the back. "I thought I was supposed to be the smart one."

"What pact?" Vale asked.

"We made a sibling pact when she was recovering from the attack." Puck perked up. "She agreed to go to administration and report Axel for harassment if he didn't leave her alone by the end of Starball season."

"Starball ended a couple of weeks ago now," Roko added. "So if she felt threatened, the magic would have forced her to seek help."

"Exactly." Tunder grinned. "He may annoy her and she might not enjoy spending time with him, but his intentions and interactions with her have been pure. If he was going to do anything to harm her, he would have done it by now, and we'd know it."

Cleon's eyes twinkled with mischief. "And not to put too fine of a point on it, but when we made the pact, we didn't specify which Starball season. So it's technically still in effect."

My mouth fell open, and I looked at each of them like the little sister whose older brothers had tricked her once again. "You guys!"

"And will be for the foreseeable future." Puck cackled, and the other three joined him.

"It's not funny," I complained, though I wasn't truly mad. They'd been tricking me into open-ended deals since we were children.

I felt Vale relax behind me. "You guys are good at this."

"Good at tricking me," I said, sticking my tongue out at Puck.

"Good at protecting you," Vale murmured. "If I'd known you had this invisible shield around you the whole time, I wouldn't have been such an asshole in my classes."

Turning, I looked up at him. "I hope you're joking."

Roko snorted. "He's not. My buddy's in Elemental Defense with him, and he told me the instructor had to douse the room with water because Vale's fire almost burned the classroom down."

"It wasn't that bad." Vale smiled sheepishly.

"They brought in fourth-year elemental earth students to restore the wood ceilings and floors."

Vale blushed, and I couldn't help but giggle. "Well, evidently, there's no reason to worry. So you can relax."

"That's the best news I've heard all day." He laughed. "Maybe we should make a mate pact. I can refine your agreement with your brothers and—"

"No," I shut that shit down. "I'm not making any more pacts unless I have time to review them with a legal adviser."

It was only after they'd left and I was alone with my thoughts that I had time to digest what they'd said. I'd forgotten about the sibling pact, and knowing it had been there but never activated by Axel made me feel lighter.

If he truly wanted me gone, he'd had plenty of time to harass me, but he never had. Not even once. I wasn't excusing his past behavior, but he hadn't said or done anything in weeks that would make me feel like my heart was being ripped out of my chest.

What he'd said to Jana at High Crest came to mind. He'd told her never to speak about me.

Axel's proximity and how he'd looked at me in class flashed before my eyes.

We will keep this professional ... if that's what you want.

What did that mean? And why was I not concerned about it and instead ... excited?

Chapter Seventeen

"Ooh, that one's nice." Callie waggled her brows.

The dress was a sparkly ice-blue full-length satin gown with sheer sequin pleats. It had camisole straps, an A-line bodice, and a V-neck that met the empire waist before sweeping out to brush the floor.

"I love it." I sighed and held out the voile overlay, allowing the crystal appliqués to catch the light. They twinkled in the dressing room, and I knew they'd be even more ethereal in the glow of candlelight at the revelry.

Callie's dress was a lavender corset-style mermaid gown. The fitted bodice was strapless with sequin embellishments that hugged her curves before flaring with godets to the sweep train. It was backless, and with her hair pulled up, you couldn't help but trace the length of her spine with your eyes.

She was gorgeous, and if she didn't find her mate at the revelry, she'd have no problem finding a date for the next one.

"We look amazing." She linked our arms together and turned us to face the mirror. "If I don't find a mate in this dress, fate is broken."

"Agreed. There is no way you'll go unnoticed. Even the moon herself won't be able to resist you."

"From the blessed daughter's mouth to the goddess's ears," she whispered, blowing a kiss to the sky.

We found matching shoes in the same boutique, then stopped by the jewelry store before sitting at an outdoor café for coffee and cake.

"Are you nervous?" Callie asked after taking a cautious sip of her double sweet white mocha latte.

I set my fork down and wiped my mouth, stalling. I wasn't sure how to put my feelings into words. "'Nervous' is a broad term."

"You're going to be alone with Axel—on purpose, for several hours, Lyra. It's okay to have mixed emotions about it."

I shrugged and took a sip of my chai tea latte. "It's weird."

"Of course it's weird. I'd be worried about you if you didn't think it was strange." She shoved a huge bite of cake in her mouth and spoke around the crumbs. "Are you scared?"

"No." I shook my head. "After being reminded of the deal I made, any lingering tension disappeared. I feel calm now."

"You feel calm?" She tilted her head, and her tone suggested she didn't believe me. "Like, totally at ease now? With Axel? Alone?" Her voice grew more and more skeptical with each added question. "Maybe I should be worried about you."

I chuckled. "If I could explain to you in a way that made sense, we'd both understand."

"Perplexia Palter says, 'to confuse is fae, to understand is divine'," she said in a mock philosophical tone.

"Confusing someone is easy, but confusing yourself requires skill," I added.

We giggled and then casually conversed about the upcoming Winter Revelry. We discussed whether to make it a date and go to dinner first. Since all the guys were coming and Brev hated the idea of being dressed up in public, we thought it would be great fun to take him out on the town.

"If we can convince him." I waved at the server to get her attention.

"Oh, leave that to me. I think he still owes me for something. If not, Jed will drag him along if he has to." She downed the rest of her drink and reached for her purse.

"I've got it." I patted her hand when the server arrived. "Can I have the check, please?"

"It's been paid for." She smiled as she collected our empty dishes. "Would you like some water?"

"No, thank you." I pulled out my wallet. "But we didn't pay yet. There must be some mistake."

"No mistake. A gentleman paid for you and your friend when he picked up his to-go order."

I looked around the café. "Who?"

"Um..." She lifted the stacked dishes and pointed across the street. "Him. He left a generous tip too. Have a wonderful day, ladies." She left before I could pry anything more out of her.

I looked in the direction she'd indicated to find Axel walking down the street, sipping from a cup and carrying a takeout bag with the café's logo stamped on the side.

I'd only seen him outside of school twice. Once at the Spring Revelry when he'd been wearing a tuxedo, and when Vale and I had seen him at High Crest.

It was a strange thing to notice, but my mind got stuck on it as I looked him over. He was wearing a long-sleeve gray shirt, distressed jeans, and sneakers. His dark blond hair was styled normally, but he had on a pair of dark sunglasses. His sleeves were bunched up on his forearms, drawing my attention to the muscles of his arms.

He turned his head, and though I couldn't see through his dark shades, I knew when our eyes locked. He gave me a tenuous nod and crossed the street.

"Lyra?" Callie's voice was quiet.

"Hm?" I watched as Axel disappeared around a corner before turning to look at my friend.

"What's happening?" She looked genuinely concerned when she asked.

I huffed out a laugh, shook my head, and shrugged my shoulders. "I have no idea."

Chapter Eighteen

"I'm going to blow off some steam while you're gone," Vale mumbled against my lips.

He'd walked me to the portal that would take my class to the Cobalt Mountain Ridge, where a cave of lunarisite gemstones was located.

Lunarisite could only be harvested where the moon's influence was particularly strong, as the gemstone was only visible at night.

I raised my brows skeptically at Vale. "And where will you be burning the air?"

I knew the mountain would be crawling with guards, and after listening to the plans my brothers had made for things I had never even considered, I was almost positive they would be there in some form or another.

"In the mountains somewhere." Vale smirked and crushed his lips to mine. When I thought he'd release me, he surprised me by lifting me and deepening the kiss.

I melted into him, wrapping myself around his body.

He held me against him long enough that the voices around us grew quiet, and when only the sounds of nature remained, a throat cleared.

"We ... have to go," Axel said. He was close enough that I could hear the discomfort in his tone.

Vale squeezed me before patting me on the butt and pulling away. "Will you give me a minute with him?" he asked.

Nodding, I stood on my tiptoes for another quick kiss. "Be nice," I whispered against his mouth.

He chuckled. "I'm always nice."

I didn't look at Axel when I broke away from Vale. I just walked in the direction of the portal and adjusted my bag to secure it against my back.

Our assignment was to go to the mountain, descend into the caves, and work together to locate the gemstone. Lunarisite was rare due to its unique properties and limited known locations, but it wasn't so scarce that allowing groups of students to go on harvesting expeditions every year as a practice exercise for their magic would deplete the resource.

Although Lunarisite was a beautiful stone commonly used in jewelry, it had other magical purposes used in technology and construction.

I watched Vale and Axel exchange words. It didn't look overly friendly, which was the opposite of what was supposed to be happening, but they weren't arguing either, so I guessed that was a plus. Axel clenched his teeth at one point and looked away, and Vale took the opportunity to get next to him, where he whispered into his ear. Then he shoulder-checked him and walked toward me.

"I'll be waiting for you when you finish." He kissed my forehead and left before I could respond.

The brush-off would've hurt my feelings, but I knew he wasn't upset with me.

"Are you ready?" Axel's voice startled me. I hadn't heard his approach, and I yelped in surprise. "You scare easily," he said, failing to hide his smirk.

"Only when people sneak up on me," I grumbled, walking toward the portal.

I heard him chuckle behind me, but I didn't stop or acknowledge it. When I arrived on the other side of the portal, I was glad to see the rest of the class was still waiting at the entrance for final instructions.

I joined the back of the line and crossed my arms. I didn't know why I was annoyed. Or maybe I didn't want to admit I was latching on to any emotion other than the excitement I was trying to bury deep down under all the fluttering butterflies in my belly.

Axel took his place by my side. His hands were in his pockets, and he looked as cool as a cucumber—even with that little smirk on his face.

"Alright, class." Professor Rootsworth amplified her voice over the chattering students. "Stick to the area you and your partner have been assigned to. You will be graded on your successful harvest and how well you work together as a team. No need to ask how I'll see, just know that I will. You have five hours. Go."

Once we were through the carved archway, the mouth of the cave looked more like a museum entrance than an underground mining site. There was a shop with souvenirs, an information desk with guides wearing matching t-shirts, and soft music with a melodic voice-over welcoming us and giving safety instructions. There were directions and illuminated walkways with over a dozen entry points leading deeper into the mountain.

"We're this way." Axel indicated with his hand.

Two other groups went the same way, and we followed behind them, but once we were through the opening, several paths split off into different directions, and we each went our separate ways.

The boardwalk ended once we found our trail, and even though the lights had dimmed, they still guided the way.

We passed through wide openings and narrow corridors, staying quiet as we descended deeper into the mountain. Eventually, we exited a tunnel and found ourselves in an enormous cavern. There were no trails or paths, just a vast space with smaller caves, glowing pools of water, stalagmites, and stalactites.

The underground chamber was large enough to fit all of Araphel's dorm buildings and still have room for a courtyard.

"Five hours isn't enough time," I marveled as I took in the view. It was so beautiful, and there were so many places to explore. I could spend days in here.

"No. It's not." Axel's deep voice echoed off the rock walls, and his gaze was already on me when I looked at him. "But it will have to be enough for now."

Logically, I knew he was speaking about the cave assignment, but the silly butterflies in my tummy were giddy anyway.

Stop it. He's only being nice because of Vale and their agreement. He rejected you, remember?

I shifted the straps on my backpack and moved to step around him. "Should we split up?"

Axel placed his hand on my stomach, stopping me. "No. We're supposed to work together, remember?" His eyes bore into me as his hand burned through my clothes.

I shuffled backward.

"Sorry." He shoved his hand into his pocket.

Looking away, I put more space between us. "Let's go this way."

He followed silently behind me as I approached an opening that looked promising. It was a bit of a walk, and we had to climb around rocks and jump over puddles of water, but there was a faint glow inside that I was hopeful about.

We crawled on our hands and knees through the tunnel until we reached a small ledge, wide enough to sit on. I dangled my feet before spinning around and hopping down into the cave.

In the middle of the space was a shallow pond not much bigger than a bathtub, glowing with bioluminescence as water dripped from the ceiling and disturbed the calm surface.

"It's beautiful, but not what we're looking for." Axel walked around the basin. As he went, he held out his hand and shifted the dirt along the retaining wall, searching for anything hidden inside.

I followed him and watched as the dirt rolled under his power before solidifying again. "How are you doing that?"

He looked at me, stepping closer. "May I?" He held his hand out but didn't move to touch me.

I was nervous, but I wanted to learn. So I tentatively lifted my hand and slipped my palm over his.

"Concentrate on the earth," he said quietly, moving our hands to hover over the soil. After stepping behind me, he adjusted our reach and whispered, "Close your eyes."

My lids slipped shut, and without my sight, my focus narrowed to where our hands were connected.

"Good." His breath warmed the shell of my ear, sending tingles down my spine.

Though I didn't touch the land physically, my magic reached out to caress the clay.

"Pay attention to the different textures," Axel said. "Notice the contrasting temperatures between rock and earth. Feel the softness of the silt, the jagged edges of minerals ... the hard stone, and the little pellets ... rolling under your fingers..."

Our breathing deepened as his voice grew quiet, and my nipples pebbled.

"You're so responsive," he murmured. His lips brushed over my skin as he spoke. "Let me in."

He slipped his fingers through mine, and I felt the gentle nudge of his magic where we were connected. Without hesitating, I opened myself and let his magic pass through me.

It was incredible. I moaned wantonly at the sensation.

"Fuck," Axel groaned, letting his head rest against mine.

I'd shared magic with my instructors and brothers, but this was different. It was magical foreplay, and my clit throbbed in time with my heartbeat.

"Axel," I whined, knowing it sounded needy. I tried to return my focus to his lesson. "Please ... what's next?"

He shifted his stance and pulled in a shaky breath, lifting his head. "Sink deeper into the sensation, sifting through the material until you can sense the individual granules. Do you feel them?"

"Yes." My lips lifted with excitement. "I feel them."

"Good." His chest rumbled against my back. I hadn't realized we were so close. "That's good. Now feel how I lift and spin them out of my way."

His magic rushed through me as it connected with the earth, forcing me to catch my breath again.

"That's it." His breathing sped up. "Just like that. Shift them around to search past their cover. Good. Now, open your eyes."

I obeyed his command, glancing at our joined hands. The earth beneath our palms was raised, and the grains spun around in an intricate dance.

"Amazing." I bent over, and the movement pushed my ass into Axel.

He grunted, and I realized his hand had migrated as he tightened his hold on my hip. He pulled back, and I didn't want to think too much about the hard length I'd bumped into, so I ignored it and focused on what he had just taught me.

"Thank you." I straightened and blinked up at him. I was so excited, and I couldn't wait to practice on my own.

He returned my grin. "You're welcome."

I turned back to the winnowing dirt, moving our hands experimentally. It took on the same liquid-like movement I'd noticed when Axel first started searching.

"You're a good teacher," I said, moving my other hand to try by myself.

He grunted at the increased power, but I was so concentrated on my task I didn't allow myself to focus on the euphoria of our combined element.

He chuckled. "I think it's more your desire for knowledge than my ability to teach, but thank you."

I shrugged. It wasn't a secret that I liked to learn. My ranking at school was evidence enough. "I like to know things."

"I know," he said quietly, squeezing my hand. "I'm going to let go now. See if you can do it on your own."

I didn't respond. I focused on our connection, but when he pulled his magic away, the only sense I lost was the warmth of his touch. I held the magic and giggled as I moved my hands around, watching the ground gurgle like bubbles in water.

Spinning, I beamed up at him. "Seriously, thank you. You're really good at this."

"You're more than capable. You have a deeper power than you let on," he said, and the words slapped me across the face.

My smile dropped, and the affection that had blossomed between us in the little hollow went cold.

Axel's face shuttered in response, and he shook his head. "Lyra, that's not... Fuck." He closed his eyes when I took a step away from him.

He knew. I didn't have to remind him of what I was thinking.

"You're weak. I can barely sense any magic from you at all. I'm a Spring Court noble. I can't be mated to a nobody female with weak magic."

"I'm sorry." He opened his eyes and looked at me with the kind of determination I'd seen when he was trying to get rid of me. "I'm so fucking sorry, Lyra."

I shook my head and backed away. "It's fine." My voice was wobbly, and I stumbled over my feet.

"No, it's not fucking fine," he ground out. "I didn't mean—" His words cut off, and he huffed in irritation. "I need you to understand. How can I make you understand?" His eyes were wide as they bounced back and forth between mine.

He looked desperate and wild, and when he paced, he reminded me of a caged animal.

"Axel?" I inched forward. I was worried, not scared. The more agitated he got, the worse the ground shook, and I didn't think they were natural tremors anymore.

"I'm sorry. I need you to understand." He stopped and looked at me, his face severe as he closed the distance. "I never wanted—" His words stopped. Then he reached out, wrapped his hands around my arms, and pulled me against him.

"Axel!" I pushed at his chest, but he didn't release me. He circled his arms around my body and held me close. He was bigger and stronger than me, and his arms were like a vise. I was trapped in his cage.

"Please trust me." He sounded defeated but unwavering. Then I felt his magic push against me. It was not the little trickle it had been a moment ago but a flood of his essence, threatening to drown me. "Let me in," he encouraged, and just like before, I complied.

It hit me all at once. I sagged against him, moaning at the onslaught. A sense of euphoria rushed through my veins, my skin flushed and my nipples perked. I was sated, like I'd had an orgasm, and my body was limp enough that he had to hold me up. My head fell to his chest, and he hugged me tightly as I listened to his heartbeat.

"You're like sunshine after the rain." His breath spilled over the crown of my head. Then he rested his head on mine. "Feel me."

Closing my eyes, I did. I felt him as he pushed his magic into me. It was as exhilarating as the last time, but there was a distinct sense of *him* beneath the surface.

Emotions that baffled me thundered through my body. Some I understood and knew well, but others were unfamiliar.

Shame and embarrassment were potent. But there was anger there—so much rage it made my chest tight. Embedded deep inside was some conflict that couldn't be put into words. It was a visceral kind of hatred I hoped to never feel for myself.

"I'm so sorry. I never..." His words stalled in his throat, but instead of silence, emotions pulsed between us. He used our connection to the earth to tell me what he couldn't seem to speak, and the regret and longing were so powerful it made my breath hitch.

"I'm sorry for everything," he whispered as I choked on a sob.

I didn't know what it meant, and he was obviously unwilling to tell me, but he allowed me to experience his feelings without explanation or context.

"Why are you sharing this with me?" I sniffled. "I don't understand. Just tell me."

"I can't." He held me tight as the ground quaked around us. "I know you don't understand. I'm not asking for anything, Lyra—"

His words cut off as we both stumbled. He kept his arms around me, but there was some distance between us now. I looked up at him in question, shielding my eyes from the falling rubble.

"I just... Can you ever forgive me?"

I felt like a bird stuck in a breeze. I couldn't move. "I..."

He shook his head and moved to steady me. “You don’t have to answer that. We should go.” He wrinkled his brow and looked around the room. “Something’s wrong. This doesn’t seem natural.”

“That wasn’t you?”

“No.” He shook his head, boosting me onto a small ledge next to the exit tunnel. But before he could pull himself up, there was a loud crack as the room trembled. He stumbled backward as rocks and dirt fell around us, choking the air with dust and debris.

As the tremors intensified, I frantically tried to channel my magic into the room, hoping to stabilize the ground, but whatever was happening was beyond my control—as if something was preventing me from doing so.

The deafening sound of fracturing stone filled the tunnel behind me as the wall crumbled and broke apart. The large cavern in the outer room collapsed, and I barely had time to close my eyes before a plume of dirt shot toward me.

“Lyra!” Axel called, but his voice seemed to come from a great distance. I saw the fear in his eyes as a shower of earth and wreckage erupted from the tunnel, hurtling towards me with deadly force.

I instinctively covered my head with my arms, but the impact was so strong that I was thrown from the ledge. I felt Axel’s arms wrap around me as he pulled me to his chest, and we fell to the ground together. The violent rumbling continued, and a wall of rock and dirt tumbled down around us.

My scream at the sudden pain was only muffled by the dark.

Chapter Nineteen

I woke to a whine, followed by a wet nudge.

Wiping my hand across my cheek, I looked up into the largest ice-blue eyes I'd ever seen. They glowed faintly in the dark, but I couldn't see anything beyond the dim light of the pond.

The air was dusty, and when I went to sit up, a sharp hurt in my leg had me sucking in a breath as I muffled a wail.

The massive wolf whimpered and pushed his muzzle against my chest.

"What are you doing?" My voice was hoarse. It could have been from the dry air we were breathing or the screams I remembered releasing before I'd passed out from the agony.

The situation obviously wasn't life-threatening since my glamour was firmly in place.

Axel angled his wolf's head down my leg. He sniffed the wound, and his chuffs of hot breath scalded my skin. I sucked in a gasp at the twinge of pain, but he didn't pull away. Instead, he looked at me and slowly opened his jaw to reveal sharp teeth.

"What—" I tried to ask, but he silenced me as he closed his teeth around my leg and ripped the fabric of my jeans away from the gash.

Before I could ask him again what he was doing, he laved my bloody leg with his tongue, cleaning the wound. If the injury hadn't hurt so much, his licks would have tickled. He cleaned the area as best he could, but the cut continued to bleed.

I wasn't sure if it was the most sanitary way to clean the wound, but I didn't think he could make it any worse. I tried to heal it, but the cut was deep, and I could only stave off the worst of it.

"Why are you shifted?" I asked.

His gaze fixed on the ceiling, and as if his acknowledgement of its presence was an invitation for the cave to respond, a rumble cracked through the cavern. Axel pounced and enveloped me with his body, pulling me beneath him to keep me safe. He huffed and grunted as rocks and chunks of dirt hit him instead of me, using himself as a barrier to protect me from the falling debris.

Drawing on my air element, I used my magic to aid him without letting him know I was using the power. I could feel the weight shift in the air when another boulder slipped free of its hold, and I subtly nudged it so it wouldn't hit him.

When the worst of it was over, he drew on his earth element to patch up the ceiling. Without thinking, I plunged my hands into his soft fur coat and opened my magic to him, allowing him to draw from my power. A deep rumbling vibrated through my hands, and I wondered if this was a wolf's version of a purr.

A wild wolf's fur was coarse, and while I suspected that Axel's was, too, his underbelly was so soft it almost felt silky. I couldn't help but run my hands over it.

I realized what I was doing when I finally noticed how quiet it was in the room. I could hear his breathing but nothing else as he held himself still.

I stopped and pulled my hands away, and instead of moving, he shifted into his fae form on top of me. It happened so fast that I sucked in a breath of surprise and reached out again, my hands landing on his bare chest.

He hovered over me with the weight of his waist and legs pressing against mine.

"Axel—"

"We need to get out of here before this entire section collapses," he said, cutting me off.

I pulled my hands from his body and covered my eyes. "Okay."

"What are you doing?"

"I... You need to get dressed."

He chuckled and gently wrapped his hand around my wrist, pulling my fingers away from my face.

"I spelled all my pants and shoes to evanesce when I shift." He smirked. "I'm not naked. You don't have to hide your eyes."

My face burned with embarrassment, and I could only hope his night vision wasn't as good in fae form as when he was a wolf.

He finished rolling off me and scooted down to my wound.

"This is bleeding again," he grumbled as he reached behind him and grabbed a tattered shred of his shirt.

"I'll just have to deal with it." I sat up and tried not to make too much of a fuss, but when I moved my leg, a yelp escaped my mouth.

"What? What's wrong?"

I sucked in a breath. "I think it's broken."

He ground his teeth together and wiped the blood from my leg, placing his other hand on my skin. A glow flared to life where we were connected, flashing over me as healing energy moved between us. The bleeding stopped, the cuts knit themselves together, and most of the discomfort disappeared. If my face looked anything like his, we were equally shocked.

"I didn't know you had healing magic," I said hopefully.

He looked at me as I stared at my leg. "I don't."

"That shouldn't be possible," I whispered.

Mates could heal each other from rudimentary injuries, but Axel wasn't my mate. My leg was probably still broken. A major injury required a skilled healer, but somehow, I was on the mend. Only a faint throbbing remained.

"That shouldn't be possible," I repeated.

I was stunned by the healing, but the look in his eyes was more surprising. He looked ... amazed. His eyes were bright with bewilderment, and the effect was overwhelming.

"I don't know if I can walk on it." I murmured.

"I will carry you," he announced, snapping to attention. "Will you power-share with me so I can get us out of here?"

"Yes. But how do we escape? Where do we go?" I wasn't confident in my ability to sense the right path through the earth. My focus was split between the injury and my frayed nerves.

I could protect myself. I could escape the tunnels anytime I wanted, but I wouldn't abandon him. I'd never leave someone behind like that, but I couldn't expose myself either. Not if there was another way.

"My earth magic is stronger than yours. I can get us out of here safely," Axel said as he took my backpack and put it on. He wasn't bragging about being more powerful than me; he was simply stating a fact. I knew he was more capable than I was with earth, just like Vale was more dominant in fire.

That was the balance.

It was the first time Axel had said something about my power that didn't leave me feeling slighted.

"I'm going to lift you. You'll need to hold on so I can use my hands and carry you at the same time."

"Okay."

Bending, he slid one arm under my knees and wrapped the other around my waist. I clung to his neck, and he lifted me, cradling me to his chest.

"Is this ... okay?"

Our faces were too close, but I didn't pull away. "Yes."

Axel still wasn't wearing a shirt, and his skin was warm. He smelled like pine needles and rain, and I wanted to bury my nose in his neck and inhale his scent.

"We need to leave now," I said, too abruptly for it to be casual.

He smirked and adjusted his hold. "We're going, sweetheart."

"Don't call me that," I grumbled.

His lips quirked into a smile. "Open your element to me so we can get out of here."

"Don't make it weird."

"I won't."

I squinted and loosened my hold on my magic.

I wished it didn't feel so good.

I involuntarily tightened my hold and he did the same, which drew us even closer than before. We were both breathing heavily, and it took a few moments for him to move, but when he did, he quickly carved a passageway into the rock on the opposite side of the cavern.

Several feet into the tunnel, the little light from the pond disappeared and we plunged into darkness.

By rights, I could see in the dark, but because my glamour hid some of my abilities, I was as blind as a bat. I was comfortable in the shadows, instinctually relaxing as darkness surrounded me like a blanket on a cold night, and as my element filled me up, it leeched away some of my tension.

"You're not scared?" Axel's voice was quiet as the earth grumbled and groaned around us.

"Why would I be scared?"

"We live in the Night Kingdom, but that doesn't mean people aren't afraid of the dark."

I snorted and laid my head on his shoulder, close enough that my forehead brushed against his neck.

"I'm not scared of the dark. I like it. Are you scared?" I didn't know if being trapped under a mountain with someone afraid of the dark was a good idea. Not that I had a choice.

The icy-blue glow of his eyes roamed over my face, and though I couldn't see his features, I knew he was smirking. "No. I'm not afraid of the dark. I've always found it welcoming."

I nodded like a fool. "That's good."

He adjusted his hold on me as we moved, and through our power-sharing connection I could sense when he moved boulders and slate walls out of our way.

"I promise I won't get claustrophobic and trap us in here," he said, picking up the conversation.

The path he'd carved left a wide space for my legs, but the other side was a tighter squeeze. Occasionally, his elbow would bump into the wall, and dirt and rocks would tumble against us. I would be cleaning clumps of clay out of my hair for weeks, but my hurt leg never jostled or hit the wall to cause me more pain.

"Thank you." I closed my eyes. I felt awkward and vulnerable, but I wanted to acknowledge his kindness.

"For what?"

"For helping me."

"I wouldn't have left you behind, Lyra."

"I know." I squirmed in his arms. Which was stupid since he was still carrying me. "But you took care of me when I couldn't take care of myself. I appreciate it."

I felt him move as if to look at me, but I kept my eyes shut.

"I would do more if I could." His warm breath tingled against my cool skin. We'd been underground for over an hour before the cavern collapsed, and the temperature in the tunnel was dropping.

"You're cold," he stated, holding me close. His body warmed under my skin like a heater. "I'm sorry. I should have thought of it sooner."

"You have fire too?" I asked, though it was obvious. The chill around us was gone, and his body was flushed with heat.

I laid my hands flat against his chest, warming my palms and fingers. I probably would have curled into him like a cat with a blanket if we weren't moving. Luckily, I had enough sense to maintain some of my dignity—not enough to keep him from teasing me, though.

"Are you warm now?" He chuckled. "Your fingers were freezing."

"You're like a portable heater," I said, flipping my hands over. "I bet I could make s'mores on your chest."

He laughed, and as he did, I bounced against him. It was the first time I'd ever heard him laugh without an edge of cruelty. The sound was happy and full of joy, not forced and mocking.

I shouldn't have felt so comfortable in his arms since he technically wasn't mine. But I did.

It was okay, though, because of the situation we were in. After feeling some of his emotions, I knew with absolute certainty that I wasn't in danger. At least, not from him. We were in a risky situation now, but I felt safe—cared for, and protected.

I didn't know what this meant for us, not that there ever had been or would be an "us". But he'd asked if I could forgive him. I would have to give it more thought now.

If he was involved with the New Night Coalition, it wouldn't matter if his remorse was as genuine as this interaction. It was unforgivable.

But until there was proof, I had to consider if forgiveness was an option.

"We're almost through," Axel said as we changed direction again.

It was still too dark to see, but I looked around anyway. "Stop."

He didn't hesitate; he did what I'd said and moved with me as my reach brought our faces closer together.

"Lyra?" His lips whispered against my skin as he murmured.

"Almost ... got it." I held up the lunarisite, allowing its glow to illuminate his face. "We passed the test."

I turned toward him, and our noses brushed. With my arm locked around his neck and our lips only a breath apart, it was easy to imagine how this might have gone another way if things had been different.

"We make a good team." He flicked his eyes to my lips and back up again. "Are you ready?"

Nodding, I tucked the stone in my front pocket and adjusted my grip on his shoulder.

"Close your eyes. I have to push through to break us free, and it will probably get dusty," he said.

I ducked my face, closing my eyes as instructed. Axel's power swelled around us until it expelled out. It wasn't as loud as when the room had been caving in on us, but it was loud and violent enough to do as he'd said it would. Dirt rained down on our heads, and as soon as chunks of rock fell from the walls, he ran us into the open air of the night.

I was surprised when we found ourselves surrounded. Dozens of students and staff stood beneath the stars, just as dirty and weary as us. There were rescue workers and Night Kingdom guards, some in uniform and some in training gear. There were healers and onlookers, and as Axel weaved toward the group, he called out for help.

"I need a healer!"

The words were barely out of his mouth when I heard Vale call my name. He appeared in moments, hovering over me as he glared at Axel.

"What happened to her? Why is she hurt? Where are you hurt? Give her to me."

"No." Axel tightened his hold. "She needs a healer."

"I can heal her."

"No, her leg is broken."

"What?" Vale roared. "Give her to me!"

"Hey, I'm fine." I kept my arm around Axel's shoulder but reached out with my other hand and placed it on Vale's chest. "It's not that bad. Axel saved me. Please calm down."

He took my hand in one of his and placed his other on my face before bending down and kissing me. "Don't ever scare me like that again."

"Yeah, he's been a real pain in the ass." Puck's voice surprised me enough that I pulled away from Vale.

Vale glared at him but stayed silent. They didn't elaborate, but I got the sense that Vale hadn't been alone in being an ass.

"I can check you two off the list now." Puck lifted a tablet and made a big show of doing his job as the Night Queen's son. "Take her to tent three. My brother, Cleon, and his mate are there. I'll let them know you're coming."

I instantly forgot about my pain at the prospect of meeting my brother's mate. I tried to contain myself, but if the twinkle in Puck's eye indicated anything, I didn't hide it very well. At least, not from him.

"Let's go." I patted Axel's chest like he was my horse, then held my hand out for Vale.

Axel smirked at me and tipped his head. "Yes, milady."

Vale didn't argue—he just took my hand and walked by my side.

Inside the tent were tables of other injured fae, but none of their wounds looked too serious. I spotted Cleon right away. He kept his cool, but our eyes locked briefly, and I saw his relief.

He came forward and acted as though we'd never met before. "Puck said you need a healer." He looked me over. "Where are you hurt?"

Axel explained everything that had happened in detail, up to the point where he'd healed me. Then he looked at me and stuttered, "A-And—"

"I healed myself as best I could," I told Cleon.

His jaw clenched. He knew I was lying to him, but I had no choice. I wasn't going to out us in the middle of a healing tent.

Axel took me to a medical table and sat me down, but before he let me go, I hugged him. "Thank you."

He wrapped his arms around my back and held me until I made a move to let go. "You're welcome, Lyra." His eyes were soft when he stepped away, tipping his head to Vale before leaving.

"We have so much to talk about, mate." Vale smirked, running his fingers down my face.

"Yes, we do," Cleon whispered low enough that no one would hear.

Little hands pushed between their arms to separate them, and a sweet voice followed. "Let me through so I can meet my patient."

Cleon smiled at me before he and Vale stepped aside, revealing my brother's mate.

"Hello, my name is Rini."

Chapter Twenty

As she drew closer, I couldn't help but feel captivated by Rini's enchanting presence. Though I'd heard so much about her, she was a mystery. Her eyes were like pools of molten amber, flickering with a depth of warmth that seemed to hold a wealth of knowledge and kindness.

She exuded a soft, feminine energy, and there was a fluidity to her movement that mirrored her healing magic. She walked with precision and care, gliding through the space gracefully.

Rini's hair was a pleasant shade of buttercream yellow, like the petals of a lily in full bloom. Soft tendrils and springy curls cascaded down her back and sat obediently around her shoulders.

Her welcoming disposition instantly put me at ease. There was a soothing reassurance about her, and not only because she was a healer in the physical sense, but as if she'd brought peace and tranquility with her presence into the room.

"You're beautiful," I blubbered as a blush stained my cheeks.

"Oh, well, thank you. You're lovely, too, even under all this dirt." She reached out and wiped a smear of mud from my face. "Let's get you fixed up."

I was star-struck. I didn't know what to say, so I bit my lip and silently followed her directions.

Once I was lying on the exam table, she held her hands over me. Starting at my head, she quickly passed over my entire body to assess the damage before she healed me.

"Did you heal yourself, Lyra?" she asked as her hands returned to my leg.

"Yes." I cringed internally. I didn't want to lie, but I had no choice. "It was bleeding, and we needed to move, so..." I let the words trail off.

Vale took my hand but said nothing. I didn't dare look at Cleon. I wasn't sure what I would find in my brother's features, and I didn't want to react in any way in front of his mate.

"You did well." Rini smiled. "It's still broken, but it's not bad for a quick fix. Ready?"

I nodded, and she went to work. It didn't hurt—if anything, it itched. Warmth seeped into my skin like rays of sun on a bright summer day. The shifting of bone and stitching of flesh should have been painful, but that was the beauty of a master healer. Their skill came with pain relief.

It was over in a few minutes, and I sighed when my leg was whole again. "Thank you," I breathed, suddenly tired.

"You're welcome." Her voice was soothing as she healed my remaining scrapes and bruises. When she got to my face, I yawned. "Have you ever needed healing before?"

"Once when I was small, and another time recently."

"Then you know you'll need rest as your body regenerates. That's why you're sleepy." She giggled as I yawned and tried to nod. "After a warm bath and a hot meal, you're going to stay in bed for the day. Doctor's orders, understand?"

I grinned. "Yes, ma'am."

She looked at Vale, and he gave her a nod. "I will make sure she is taken care of, and leave with her as soon as you finish."

"Good. Then you may take her." She glanced at me again. "It was a pleasure to meet you, Lyra. Get well soon."

"Thank you," I replied, wishing I could say more.

When her back was to me, my brother caught my eye.

"I love her," I whispered to him.

"So do I." He gave me a wink before trailing behind her as they went to her next patient.

I couldn't wait to talk to him and tell him how wonderful I thought his mate was. I couldn't wait to meet her properly and tell her myself.

Vale scooped me up and cradled me against him. I rested my cheek on his shoulder, and he kissed my head as he moved toward the door.

"Your family knows you're safe."

"How do you know?"

"We're in a group chat. Puck told them as soon as he sent us to see the healer."

I chuckled at his excitement.

"Good luck with that. Your phone will never be quiet again."

He snorted. "I've noticed. They all want to see you but agreed you need rest first."

"I'm sure they're busy with all this too." I knew my entire family would be nearby. It wasn't just my brother's duty to be here, but my parents' as well. They were the most powerful fae in the Night Kingdom, and their skills would be useful.

People were shouting outside the tent, which wasn't surprising, but it was louder than when I'd arrived. "What's going on?"

"I don't know." Vale furrowed his brow. "I'll try to go around."

A crowd had gathered at the cave entrance, forming a loose circle around a tall, well-dressed male. He was talking animatedly to those I quickly recognized as reporters. They held up recording devices, taking pictures of him as he spoke to the onlookers.

When I looked around, my eyes locked with Axel's. He held himself rigid as he stood off to the side of the male I recognized as Azael Stonebrook—a member of the Spring Court Council and, more importantly, Axel's father.

Axel looked away. He'd cleaned up and found a shirt, but the dirt on his skin made it obvious he'd been inside the cave.

"There she is now," Azael said, raising his voice over the chatter.

I didn't realize Axel's father was talking about me until the crowd surrounded us. Lights, cameras, and microphones were shoved in my face. The reporters asked dozens of questions all at once, not giving me enough time to answer before shouting another.

"Give us the details of how you were injured!"

"Share with the realm how the Spring noble rescued you."

"Tell us what happened inside the cave."

"What's your name?"

"How do you know Axel Stonebrook?"

"Is it true you attend Araphel together?"

"Are you close with the Spring noble?"

"Friends, calm down," Azael said, appearing at Vale's side. He held up a hand to the curious journalists. "One question at a time, and give her a chance to speak." He plastered on a bright smile, and the crowd ate it up.

"I will answer your questions," Axel stated, stepping closer as if to position himself between us and the reporters.

But Azael promptly placed his hand on Axel's shoulder, giving it a hard squeeze, and pulled him to his opposite side.

"Nonsense." Azael's face hardened before returning to a pretentious charm. "You'll have your chance, so let the young woman speak. Reed, please ask your question again," he told a short, thin male with glasses, then turned to look at me. Whatever charm the crowd saw in his eyes, I did not.

I shrank under his powerful gaze. There was nothing warm in his smile, nothing friendly or encouraging about him. He looked mean. Hollow, even.

"Miss, what is your name?" Reed asked.

Vale shook his head at the crowd. "Statements will have to wait—"

"Her name is Lyra, isn't that right, dear?" Azael interrupted, raising his brows at me while ignoring the glare he received from Vale. I was sure he'd meant it to look encouraging, but his dominance overwhelmed me. His intensity held me captive, and I nodded in answer.

When Azael glanced back at the crowd, I pushed my face into Vale's chest.

"Excuse us." Vale tried again to step forward, but the reporters wouldn't budge.

"Tell us, Lyra, how the Spring noble came to rescue you."

"Is it true that you would have died without his help?"

"I said statements will wait," Vale shouted.

A tall female leaned over Reed and shoved her recorder in my face. "You'd still be trapped down there if not for the Spring noble. Would you care to make any comment about your rescue?"

I patted Vale on the arm, knowing I had to say something to get us out of there. "What's your name?" I asked the female.

"Penrose," she replied without missing a beat. "Tell us how the Spring noble rescued you."

"That is quite enough," my mother's voice rang out loud and clear over the crowd.

An audible hush fell over the crowd as everyone bent at the waist or dipped into a curtsy. The microphones and cameras disappeared, and the flashing lights stopped.

"My Queen." Azael barely inclined his head as he addressed her. "The people are due an explanation about what happened here. They are also interested in the young female my son rescued."

My mother didn't acknowledge Azael with words. She placed herself in front of the crowd with my fathers, hiding me from view.

"My esteemed members of the press, your eagerness to uncover the truth is commendable, and we share your sentiments. Rest assured that, when appropriate, we will provide you with the information you require. Nonetheless, I must remind you that this is a rescue site, and our focus remains on the well-being of those trapped during the earthquake. Your patience and cooperation are expected so that our medical staff and rescue workers can perform their duties effectively. You must also carry out your responsibilities with the utmost care and exercise empathy when conducting your interviews. Our students and faculty have been subjected to a traumatic experience. I implore you to grant those affected by this tragic event the time and privacy needed to recover."

She was polite as she castigated their behavior. Maybe I would have been able to muster up a fraction of her poise if I'd been in the right headspace, but listening to her address the crowd, I knew I had decades to go before I could fill her shoes.

They quietly acquiesced, apologizing and thanking her simultaneously.

"Thank you for your understanding," she said, directing them to where they were supposed to be as they waited for answers in the makeshift press gallery.

As the journalists shuffled off, Azael moved toward my parents.

"I'm sure our generous Queen wouldn't mind if I gave a statement about my brave son and his daring rescue." He shifted his gaze toward my mother, causing several reporters to pause. "After all, he saved a young fae's life this evening. With the Winter Mating Revelry next week, the people might be interested in learning more about the noble bachelor and his attendance."

The tension around us ratcheted up in an instant. Vale stiffened, and though my parents didn't react, I knew them well enough to sense the change in the air.

Azael's oily smile was suspicious, but the way he briefly flicked his eyes to mine was far more troubling.

"Imagine if he was given a worthy mate at the event. What a wonderful blessing that would be, especially after such a heroic feat."

A low growl rumbled in Vale's chest, and I used our connection through the mating bond to reassure him. We had to tread carefully, and his reaction wouldn't benefit any of us.

Was Azael fishing or simply testing the waters?

One thing was for sure—he knew I was the one his son had rejected.

"Councilmen Stonebrook." My mother's sweet, regal voice was slightly louder as she responded to him. I had to bite back a smile at her tone. Azael may have thought he was clever, but he had nothing on Queen Hesper. "I have no objection to you speaking with the press. In fact, I wholeheartedly agree with and encourage it. I think they'd find his story fascinating, don't you agree?"

Azael's smarmy smile slipped, but she continued speaking, even as she casually stepped closer.

"Perhaps when I make an official statement, I'll include your son's courageous actions. After all, the people have the right to hear about him and know the truth. Until then, I'll leave it in your capable hands."

He froze, turning red, but she didn't give him the opportunity to respond. She turned her back on him, gave me a cursory once-over, and shifted into her Nightshade form, slipping into the darkness with my fathers in tow.

Chapter Twenty-One

"Your mom is a fucking badass," Vale said for the third time.

I was sprawled on his chest as he held me in our large bathtub the morning after our interaction with Axel's father. When we'd arrived home the previous night, he had to wake me so I could shower before bed. If I hadn't been covered in dirt and mud, I would have argued, but my skin was gritty, and when he'd helped me out of my clothes, chunks of clay and rock fell to the floor.

This morning, he'd surprised me with breakfast in the bath, which I hadn't realized was one of my favorite things until now. He kept the water toasty warm with his fire element and opened the window to balance the heat and humidity, which led to another discovery. Outside the window, climbing up the entire back wall of our dorm and crawling over my bedroom and bathroom windows, were my favorite pink vining geum smoke flowers. They had a slightly sweet scent, but the fragrance was so subtle and delicate that few noticed it. I loved them. I didn't know why they were growing on my building, but I was excited to put them in vases around our rooms.

"When can I see your Nightshade form?"

I ducked my head. This wasn't something we'd talked about.

"Why are you blushing?" He gave me a curious smile. "What don't I know, my mate?"

I pressed my forehead to his chest. "It's embarrassing."

He didn't let me hide, though. He sat up, adjusting my legs until I straddled him, sloshing water onto the floor.

"You are safe with me, Lyra. You know that, don't you?"

"I know." Running my hands over his chest, I averted my eyes. "It's nothing, really. It's just… I'm meant to be queen one day and…"

"And what?" He tucked his finger under my chin and tilted my head. "Tell me."

"I don't have full control of my shifted form."

"That's nothing to be embarrassed about." He kissed my nose. "The more powerful the form, the harder it is to control."

I shrugged. I knew that. "If only it were just that. I'm not allowed to fully shift into my Nightshade form unless it's an emergency."

"Well, that makes sense." Vale's brows pulled down. "Why is that embarrassing?"

Biting my lip, I looked away and huffed. He'd find out sooner or later, so I may as well admit to it. "I startle easily."

"I've noticed." A small grin lifted his lips. "Is that… Does that mean you…"

"Poof into a ball of smoke when I get scared? Yes." I buried my face in my hands, dropping forward to lean on him.

My head bounced against his chest as he tried and failed to hide his laughter.

"It's not funny. It's mortifying," I whined.

Vale's arms circled me as he peppered me with kisses. "You're so fucking adorable."

"See! That's why it's embarrassing. I'm supposed to be a Queen someday, not some cutesy fae who poofs into a cloud."

"You're just making it sound more precious."

I snorted. "If it weren't me, I might agree."

"So if I were to sneak up on you?"

I shook my head before he finished the thought. "The geas won't allow it. I literally can't fully shift unless it's to save my life. And jump scares don't count."

He belted out a hearty laugh, and I had to admit, it was a little funny, so I laughed with him.

"Well, we need to get you some more mates to lift that geas. I have ideas." He winked. "You can partially shift, though?"

"I kept my wings, but again, I'm not supposed to use them."

"But you can control them?" His brows lifted with his excitement. "Can I see?"

My back tingled at the prospect, and my eyes flicked to the open windows. Before I could close them myself, Vale's air magic rolled through, slamming them shut and pulling at the humidity to fog the glass. When he finished, we were ensconced in what looked like a fluffy white cloud.

His voice dropped as he ran his fingers down my spine. "Now can I see?"

I arched at his touch and sighed as I released my wings. Feeling them unfurl after not using them for so long was amazing. It wasn't uncomfortable to keep them hidden, not like how a muscle became sore from disuse, but it still felt good to stretch them out.

They were dark against the white haze of the bathroom, and the contrast was beautiful. Vale watched with obvious wonder, reaching out to touch them as if he couldn't help himself. I wasn't used to being admired like this, but I loved it and my wings fluttered at his rapture.

He sucked in a breath when he made contact. "They're not solid." He sounded awed.

His surprise was understandable. It wasn't as if there were many of us around. Most fae would never see my Nightshade form in person, and even fewer would get this close.

"They're a manifestation of the darkness, not flesh and bone."

"They feel like ... I don't know, water and air?"

I turned to watch as he stroked his fingers over my smokey wings. They were solid, but they acted like liquid. He manipulated the ethereal substance, tracing patterns across the surface. They seemed to respond to his every touch, pulsing and undulating with energy that was both beautiful and arousing.

"What does it feel like?" he murmured as he trailed his fingers through the wispy extensions.

"Like you're running your fingers through my hair. Only better." Closing my eyes, I leaned forward. "It feels good." I moaned, and when I shifted again, I slid over his hard shaft.

Vale slipped his hand up my neck and fisted my hair, turning my head to kiss me. My nipples pebbled, and I mewled into his mouth. Releasing my wing, he wrapped his arm around my waist and stood from the bath, spilling more water onto the floor and making an even bigger mess.

"Don't put them away," he ordered as he stomped to the bedroom, keeping us hidden in the fog. His hold on the mist would dissipate without the water, but our bedroom had been spelled for privacy so I could keep them out without the risk of someone seeing.

He sat on the bed, pressing his back against the headboard. "I want to watch you, and next time, I'm bending you over," he announced as he angled his cock and gently pulled me down onto him.

The water from the bath thinned my silky arousal and made him feel bigger than he already was, but I was desperate for him all the same, rolling my hips impatiently. He kept his hands around my waist and moaned as I worked myself onto him. Vale took shallow breaths, his stomach pulled in, and his hips pushed out for a better angle. When he was fully seated, I rested my hands on his chest and ground my pelvis into his.

"Fuck," he groaned, sliding his hands up to cup my breasts and thumb the tips.

Sitting up, he ducked his head and took one nipple into his mouth, then the other, flicking the hardened nubs with his tongue before kissing up my neck. Releasing my breasts, Vale ran his hands around my back and palmed the edges of my wings.

The added contact was overwhelming as every nerve in my body lit up with pleasure. Wrapping my arms around his neck, I lost myself to the stimulation.

It was loud and vigorous. We were still wet from the bath, but the sex was sweaty, and our skin was hot. I moaned as Vale cursed and jerked beneath me. He roared, following me over the edge as an orgasm overtook me, then toppled onto the bed, taking me with him.

Vale lazily ran his fingers up and down my back after I'd evanesced my wings away, and we laid there for long enough that the room cooled and our bodies became clammy.

"We need another shower," I mumbled against his chest.

"I need more energy so we can do that again."

I chuckled, kissing his neck, and as I slid up his body, his softening cock slipped out of me.

He groaned and twitched under me. "Definitely need more energy," he mumbled into my mouth.

"Let's get you fed then." I rolled off the bed and headed to the shower.

An hour later, Vale and I walked hand in hand through the courtyard to the entrance gates, aiming for the portal hidden in a secret alcove nearby. Over the sidewalk leading us from our dorm to the courtyard, someone had grown a canopy of purple wisteria, brightening my already cheerful mood. The sweet floral scent filled the air, and I loved them almost as much as the geum smoke flowers.

The sun was bright, the birds were chirping happily, and the grass looked greener than the day before.

"I wonder if this is someone's assignment," I said with a happy sigh.

Vale shrugged. He didn't have an affinity for earth like I did, so he wasn't as excited about the new growth.

"Maybe." He reached out, plucked a white rhododendron flower from the bush next to the gate, and put it in my hair. "But whoever did it, I hope they get an A for putting this smile on your face."

"It was for you first." I tugged him down for a kiss.

Vale hummed against my lips before tucking his nose against my neck. "You smell even sweeter than normal. We should find whomever did this."

I giggled and pulled away. "Why?"

"So they can make us a bed of flower petals, and I can spread you out and suckle on that sweet puss—"

A throat cleared, cutting off Vale's words. Axel stood on the path ahead, close enough to hear what Vale had been saying, and his sheepish grin was proof.

"Sorry, I didn't mean to interrupt."

"That's usually the intended purpose of clearing one's throat," Vale told him dryly. "Don't eavesdrop, you dick."

Axel smirked at Vale as he held up his hands. "It was an honest mistake."

"Doubtful, you lurker. What do you want?" Vale's words were dismissive, but his tone was friendly. Either he was faking it like a master, or this was a glimpse of what their friendship used to be like.

As much fun as it was to watch them interact, my face was still hot from the conversation he'd walked in on, and I shifted around nervously. A strange dynamic was developing between us, and it confused me.

Axel turned his full attention to me and gave me a once-over like he was looking for anything out of place. "How are you feeling?"

"I'm fine."

His lips twitched as he fought a grin. "How's your leg?"

"Oh." I looked down, flustered. "It's perfectly healed, and I finally washed all the dirt off too." I ran my fingers through my hair, accidentally knocking the flower loose.

Axel snatched it out of the air, stepping forward, and tucked it behind my ear.

"I'm glad." His voice was softer, and his hand lingered against my skin. "I also want to apologize for my father's behavior."

He met my eyes briefly, then backed away and shoved his hands in his pockets.

"Yeah, what the fuck was that about?" Vale tucked me under his arm. "Does he know—" He cut himself off and looked down at me.

"He was there," Axel admitted.

"Your dad's a fucking asshole, Ace." Vale's friendliness had vanished. "Why are you—" He stopped and shook his head. "We've got to go."

"Why am I what?" Axel stepped in front of Vale to stop us from leaving.

Shaking his head, Vale grabbed Axel's arm and moved him aside. "Forget it. I'm not rehashing this with you. You made your choice."

"That's the thing about choices, Vale," Axel called as we walked away. "Sometimes, they're taken away from you."

His words stopped us in our tracks, and we turned around.

Axel was angry, but defeat flashed through his eyes. He focused on me when he spoke. "I'm sorry for what was said. He had no right. I'm glad you're feeling better." He gave me a small smile, then turned and walked away.

Chapter Twenty-Two

"Finally!" Puck threw his hands in the air and shook his head. "We've been waiting all damn day."

My family was in the living room when Vale and I arrived at the castle's private quarters. There was a buffet-style setup of food and drinks on the counter, and they all had small plates in their hands.

"We're not that late." I rolled my eyes at Puck as my mother stood to greet me.

"We must run on different time then, Lala. You were supposed to be here two hours ago."

I ignored him, focusing on my mother and letting Vale take over the annoying-brother situation. In the few weeks Vale and I had been together, he'd quickly found a place of his own with my brothers, and sometimes that place included running interference with Puck. They knew each other since we all went to school together, but Puck and Roko also had a mated dorm room in the same building, and we spent a lot of time with them after classes and dinner.

"Hi, sweet girl." My mother hugged me tight. "Even with your abilities and the precautions we took with the necklace, I worried about you. How are you really, Lyra? You went through something very traumatic."

"I'm okay." I pulled away to look at her. "Truly. It was scary and I was hurt, but I'm fine. I wasn't alone, so that helped."

"Yes, but you were trapped with him for hours." She gave me a sad smile.

"Actually, Axel was great." A hush fell over the room. Everyone turned toward me. "Don't look at me like that." I faced them, keeping my arm wrapped around my mom's waist since she didn't seem inclined to release me. "His ill-mannered father was right about one thing—Axel saved my life."

I proceeded to tell them everything that occurred in the cavern—how I'd thought it was him making the room shake, and when we'd realized that something else was happening, it was too late.

I'd already given Vale a more thorough breakdown of my time with his former best friend, and there were things I was leaving out in my story to my family, but they were getting all the crucial details.

"He shifted to protect you?" Cleon shook his head. "That's ... odd."

"Why?" I asked, popping a grape in my mouth.

"That's mate behavior. Guarding you. Cleaning your wound."

"Healing you," Tunder added with raised brows. "We're free to speak about that now, baby sister. We know you didn't heal that leg on your own."

Baba leaned forward in his chair. "He's not a healer. That shouldn't have been possible."

I shrugged. "That's what I thought, too, but he did. I'm assuming it's because of the remnants of the bond still lingering between us."

"None of it makes sense." Father sipped his whiskey. "We're missing something. You shouldn't have remnants. He shouldn't have been able to heal you or claim you—and let's be honest, that's what he did in animal form."

"In a limited way, yes," Pai agreed.

Baba nodded. "It is consistent with pack mentality. Obviously, shifting to defend and protect someone is within reason. Any of us would have done the same," he said, wafting his hand to my parents and brothers. "But I'm inclined to agree that it was more with him. I would have shifted into my wolf's form to protect someone, but I wouldn't have cleaned their wound. That instinct is reserved for my mate, and my family if necessary."

"Not to mention, the healing," Tunder added. "It's simply not possible. We all know this, but I asked Rini if she knew of any instances where that rule went out the window. She said there was no evidence to support that it had ever been possible."

"It makes no sense." Shea stood and paced the room. "We all watched him reject the mating bond."

"Unless he didn't," Vale said, and then it was his turn to have everyone focus on him.

"What the hell are you talking about?" Puck snapped. "We've all heard what he's said and done. We were there, Vale."

Vale shook his head, grabbing me and settling me on his lap. "No one has answers. This has never happened before."

"That we know of." Cleon raised his brows. "But go on."

"What if there's more to it than just saying the words?" Vale continued. "What if he didn't believe them?"

Vale and I looked at each other as the others mumbled to themselves.

Then it hit me.

"Or what if he didn't have a choice?" I asked.

Vale's brows raised. "He said, 'That's the thing about choices. Sometimes, they're taken away from you.'"

"When did he say that?" Father asked.

Vale's features shifted into a look of deep concentration. If anyone could read between the lines of Axel's cryptic words, it was him.

"Today, right before we came here. We saw him as we were leaving Araphel. He asked about my leg and how I was feeling." When I said this, my parents glanced at each other. "Then he apologized for his dad."

"Axel apologized for Azael?" My mother tilted her head. "Apologized for what, exactly? Did he say?"

Nodding, I ran my hand over Vale's arm. "He said he was sorry for his behavior."

"Nothing else?" Her eyes pinched with the question.

"No. Nothing else. Why?"

She looked at my fathers, then gave Shea a nod. He came over and took the chair next to me.

"We don't exactly have proof, but we believe the earthquake at Cobalt Mountain wasn't natural. Our working theory is that it was a planned attack led by members of the New Night Coalition."

Vale tightened his arm around me and sat up higher. "I'm not disagreeing, but we're all assuming Azael is part of this group, correct?"

"Yes." My family said in unison.

"Why would he lead an attack knowing his son was in there? Azael is a piece of shit, but whatever his angle, it must include Axel. Axel could have been hurt or killed."

Shea looked at me and then back to Vale. "Unless he knew."

"No." I shook my head. "I don't believe that."

"Why not?" Puck stood and put his hands on his hips. "Don't get soft on him now just because he licked your wounds."

"That's enough," Father snapped. "Do not disrespect your sister. Be angry, Puck, but keep it pointed in the direction it belongs."

Puck's arms dropped, and he bowed his head in shame before sitting back down. "Sorry, Lala. I'm unwilling to believe he's the good guy, even though he saved your life."

"Why don't you think he was involved?" Papa asked. His voice was encouraging and comforting, as always, which made it easier to open up.

"When we power-shared, he let me feel his emotions, and when the earthquake started, he was distracted as he tried to reason with me. He wasn't faking that. He has deep-rooted anger, but nothing he shared with me felt malicious. And now..." I looked at Vale. "After what he said today, I wonder if something else is going on."

Pai gave me a smile and looked at my other dads. "It's worth considering. He could have been hiding things from her, but we shouldn't rule out that he was innocent—at least in knowing about the earthquake."

"Agreed," Father said. "I'm still inclined to believe that his involvement wasn't a coincidence, though."

"Azael wasted no time calling reporters and using them for PR," Mother said. "It is interesting timing." She raised her brows at her mates. "And he played his hand perfectly."

They all nodded, as did my brothers, but I was confused. "What hand is that?"

"He was informed several days ago that Axel was not invited to the Winter Revelry. To say he was upset would be an understatement," my mother replied. "Two days later, there was a headline-grabbing seismic event that our elemental geologists didn't detect, a noble son caught in the fray, and a proud father boasting about his son's heroics in the face of a catastrophic event."

"It reeks of a setup," Puck muttered sarcastically.

Baba drummed his fingers on his leg, and his eyes pinched in concentration. "And leaves us with more questions than answers."

Cleon stood and stretched. "If only our informant would actually inform us of something. The hints, subtle messages, and warnings aren't enough to go on."

"At least it's something." Shea shoved him as they both went for more food. "Ass."

"Piss off. Those sausage rolls are mine. You've already had half a dozen."

"I'm bigger than you. I need more than you do."

"You're a bigger jackass."

"Dick."

"Jerk."

I snorted, and while they were bickering, I used my air magic and brought one of the sausage rolls to me.

Cleon turned as I snatched it out of the air. "Hey!"

"I haven't had any," I said before taking a huge bite.

"Ha." Shea took the last one, hopped over the back of the couch, and got busy eating. "Snooze, you lose, brother."

"That's not even cool. You know those are my favorite." Cleon stacked his plate with mince pies, scones, and cupcakes.

"They're everyone's favorite, you big baby." Tunder reached out and snatched a cupcake from his plate.

"So what's the plan for the ball, then?" Puck asked, acting more mature than usual as my other brothers descended into adolescence. "With Azael making a big deal about his bachelor son being at the Winter Revelry, is Lyra going or not? We had plans for everyone to attend."

My mother looked at me with a sad smile. "He's backed us into a corner with his stunt. If he insists on going and not heeding my warning, you'll have to sit this one out."

"Unfortunately, with him making it so public, he'll win this round. But only because we didn't know how he'd play this." Father took my mother's hand. "We've got something in mind for the future. If he wants to keep scheming, we'll put an end to it. He won't mess with the crown and get away with it."

"We won't tolerate these antics," Papa added.

"You two kids will just get more time to yourselves." Pai smirked at Vale. "I'm sure you'll manage."

"Your friends are still invited to go with Puck and Roko, though. Tunder, Cleon, and their mates will be there, and Shea and his mate will stand with us in support," my mother said. "You two will dress and wait here until the last minute for a final decision."

"Beyond that, we'll discuss these new developments with our trusted advisors and inform you of anything you need to be made aware of," Father said. "I'll speak with Ranehall."

"The Night Court's legal counsel? Why?" I wrinkled my brow. "He's not a general. He's not even active in the guard."

"No, but he is my protégé." Determination radiated from Father's demeanor, his voice resolute. "The Ranehalls are loyalists, and I trust him completely."

Papa nodded. "We discussed placing him under the geas after the invitation arrived addressed to you."

"We were going to wait to mention it until after the revelry though," Pai said.

"The stakes are high, and we need allies we can rely on. He has proven himself time and again, demonstrating unparalleled dedication," Baba added.

"If there's anyone I would trust with confidential access, it is him," Mother agreed.

"You've heard of his reputation, Lyra." Shea smirked. "He's the one who came up with the theory about Azael and the earthquake. He has a good sense about these things."

The infamous Queen's Counsel was known for being a hard-ass who rarely lost. He represented the Crown and, alongside my father, he served as the lead prosecutor for criminal offenses committed against the realm. His involvement was more than justified. I was just surprised to hear my father admit that he wanted to grant him access to our inner circle.

I'd never met him, but I had heard the female staff whisper about him for years, although none of them here had ever been lucky enough to be involved with him. Apparently, he had a strict rule against mixing business and pleasure. But if he did take you to bed, it was with the understanding that it was a one-time occurrence and only sex. I had seen him in the media, via photographs and videos, and heard rumors about his private interactions, so it didn't take a genius to understand their acceptance of such an arrangement.

"I trust you to know what's best," I told my parents. "If bringing him in is going to help us, I have no objection." I looked at Vale.

"I'm still finding my footing, relying on your experience and guidance. But I am fully supportive of anything that protects my mate and ends this group."

"Then it's settled," Father announced. "Following the winter ball, we'll bring Ranehall into our fold."

"In the meantime, you should reach out to Axel," Tunder told Vale. "He remains our primary candidate for gathering information."

I wondered if Axel would open up to me again. It felt wrong to use him for information, but we needed to discover if he knew something that could be dangerous to the realm. And if there was more going on with him, if his father was using him, we needed to find out.

I had to know if Axel was a victim in all of this, and if he was, I resolved to help him.

Chapter Twenty-Three

As the week went on, neither my parents nor my brothers learned anything new, and no other information about the earthquake came to light. For everyone outside of the core group, it appeared to be an anomalous natural disaster.

Azael's interview spread like wildfire, generating buzz about the Spring noble's presence at the Winter Revelry. Even though the females at Araphel had been attending school with him for the last couple of years—or longer, in some cases—and had attended mating revelries with him previously, they were thrilled at the prospect of bonding with Axel. They became convinced that the mate magic cast by the High Priestess would somehow create a connection with him that hadn't been there before. Which was ridiculous.

Hearing all the chatter had my stomach in knots. Thankfully, he wasn't participating and flirting with his admirers, but that didn't stop them from fawning over him.

I was glad he skipped our classes that week. I didn't know how much more I could take.

"I'll be so fucking glad when this stupid dance is over," Sidric complained, slamming his dinner tray on the table. "If I have to hear one more time about how *brave* and *sexy* Axel fucking Stonebrook is, I'm going to barf."

Callie snickered as I tucked my head. I wanted to laugh. I truly did. But I couldn't.

"Sorry, honey," Sidric said, and Vale cleared his throat.

"Fuck off, dude, it's just a nickname."

Vale snorted. "You're lucky I like you, or I'd knock your ass into next week."

Sidric stabbed his fork into his potatoes and used the bite to punctuate his statement. "I wish we could skip right over this shit."

"The dance is tomorrow. You can manage another day." Callie smiled sweetly. "Besides, you might find a mate. You wouldn't want to miss that!"

"I'll find my mate when the time is right. Until then, Vale, would you mind?" He turned his face and pointed to his temple. "Right here ought to flatten the mattress through the weekend."

"Tempting." Vale shook his head and brushed his lips over mine. "But I promised my mate I wouldn't murder her exes—and as I said before, I like you."

"Your loss. If I vomit on your shoes, you'll only have yourself to blame," Sidric said around a mouthful.

When the males finished shoveling food into their mouths, they left to go bro out in the gym. Callie and Jed went to the lab after taking another tissue swab from my mouth, and I headed to the library.

As I walked down the hall near my Econ class, I came across Professor Warrock locking up for the night.

"Ms. Bruadar." He smirked at me.

"Professor." I greeted him. "You're working late."

"If your peers were as studious as you, I wouldn't have to," he remarked.

"That sounds a lot like job security to me." I chuckled at him.

"Potato, potahto." He winked. "May I walk you somewhere?"

I shook my head. "I won't keep you. I'm just headed to the library. Will we see you at the revelry?

"I will be there in an official capacity, yes." He nodded before we bid each other goodbye.

Professor Warrock had been drawn deeper into my parents' inner circle because he was aware of my identity and had been placed under the geas. Due to his position at the school, he had access to a range of diverse opinions and gossip among the student body. This proved valuable, especially considering that other noble families were now coming under suspicion.

I was barely around the corner when I was grabbed and pulled into an empty classroom. I should have been startled, but I'd been pulled into that particular room a few times before, and I recognized Axel's scent.

"What are you doing?" I grumbled. "You know you can talk to me now like a normal person, right? You don't have to kidnap me."

Axel smirked. "Do you have a penchant for being dramatic, or is this special just for me?"

Rolling my eyes, I put my books on an empty desk and crossed my arms over my chest. "I'm not dramatic."

"Sure." His smile grew. Then he leaned against the door and kicked one foot over the other. "So ... what are you reading?"

Wrinkling my brow at the odd question, I looked at the two books. "*The Fae Condition* and *Anarchy, Realms, and Utopia*."

"Light reading, then." He came over and flipped through the text. "Do you ever let that brain of yours rest?"

"It's for a class." I took the book out of his hands and ducked my head to catch his eye. "Is this why you pulled me in here?"

Shoving his hands in his pockets, he sighed and shook his head. "No. I'm stalling as I rethink my actions."

"What?"

"Vale stopped by my room last night."

When he paused, I shrugged, urging him to continue.

"He asked me what I was doing tomorrow," he finally admitted.

Any trace of humor between us disappeared in a heartbeat.

"I see." I shoved the books in my bag and busied myself with the buckles.

Axel reached out and put his hand over mine. "Lyra."

"And what did you tell him?" I asked, pulling my hand free. I didn't want to discuss this with him, but if he insisted, he definitely couldn't be touching me. That was entirely too much sensory overload.

"Lyra," he repeated, his tone pleading.

Our eyes met, and tension filled the room. My chest felt tight, but I needed to know what was happening.

"You have another mate?" The statement fell from his lips like a glass slipping from his grasp. The destruction was inevitable. It crashed against the surface, piercing my ears and sending shard fragments scattering, ripping through the tenuous relationship we had.

We locked eyes for an extended moment, and as his curiosity faded into a plea, all I could offer was a simple nod. He pinched his lips and looked down, clenching his jaw. I thought he would punch the wall when he spun on his heel and raised his fist. Instead, he tapped it against the wood hard enough to make a sound but not damage his knuckles.

"Is it..." He cleared his throat and shoved his hands into his pockets. "Is it because of what I did?" His voice was quiet, and when he looked at me, he was guarded.

His question confused me. It was so open-ended. He'd done so many things—how could I possibly know which way to answer? "I'm not sure what you mean."

Turning to face me, he clarified, "Do you have more than two mates, or—" He pulled in a deep breath, steeling himself before continuing, "Are you ... replacing me?"

The question broke something within me.

It had been unfair of him to ask and even crueler to expect an answer. I couldn't help but feel frustrated. It was as if he enjoyed torturing me. His recent change in behavior had been obvious, and I couldn't ignore the longing looks anymore. But this? How dare he ask me such a question.

"Replace you? You rejected me, Axel," I said, my voice shaking with emotion.

He winced, and guilt marred his expression, but he didn't deny it. "I know ... I..."

"Aren't you going to the revelry yourself?"

"Yes, but—"

"Are you not the most 'eligible bachelor in the Night Realm'?" I asked, a note of betrayal creeping into my voice without my permission.

"No."

"The 'heroic Spring noble who saved the poor common girl's life'," I pressed on, unable to stop the words pouring from my mouth.

"That's not—"

"I can't even walk down the quad without hearing a dozen females fantasizing about the revelry. It's been one dreamy wish after another. They're all praying the High Priestesses's magic will reveal you as their mate."

"Stop."

"Perhaps if you see them in their pretty gowns, you'll finally notice them. But they don't know what I know, do they?"

"Stop it."

"They don't know that none of them are good enough. They'll never be good enough."

"Lyra." His voice lowered with a tinge of warning.

"They don't know that there's only one person who could ever possibly be good enough for you."

"That's not true—"

"But even she's not good enough. She never was and never will be because the person you created in your head doesn't exist." I sucked in a breath and covered my mouth, failing to hold back a sob.

He wavered momentarily before he pulled me against him, wrapping his arms around me and crushing me to his chest. Tears spilled down my cheeks, soaking into his shirt.

He held me so tight I felt whole again.

"You have no right to ask me that when you're going yourself." My voice was a sodden whisper between us, but he'd heard me.

He rested his forehead against my hair and shook his head. "It's not the same."

"How so?"

"Because I don't want to go." His words were hard and decisive, but his anger wasn't directed at me.

Pushing out of his hold, I stepped back and wiped my face. I hesitated before continuing, but I needed to know what he'd meant.

"Why not? Wasn't that the whole point, Axel?"

He looked taken aback. "No."

"*You* wanted someone else. Not me," I admitted. My voice cracked beneath the pain. I had no reason to be, but I was embarrassed to confess that I'd wanted him. I would have accepted him without a second thought. "You did this."

His expression was somber, and the pain in his eyes was palpable. "I know."

I winced at his admission. "It's not your place to ask me about my mates." My voice was a little stronger even as my eyes swam. "Especially when you are the one who is actively doing the replacing."

Axel shoved his hands in his pockets and stared at the floor. He cleared his throat, sniffling as I wiped my cheeks.

There was a heaviness in the room as if the air itself held weight. In spite of it being stuffy and hot, my skin felt cold as a shiver coursed through me.

Axel scuffed his shoe against the floor and shuddered on an exhale. "I shouldn't have asked," he whispered. Pinching the bridge of his nose, he swiped his thumb under his eyes before looking up at me. "I'm sorry, Lyra."

Swallowing hard, I bit my lip to stop it from quivering. My resolve eroded, and even though it was none of his business, I couldn't leave him without an answer. I wasn't sure if it made me weak, but I didn't want the question lingering between us. I didn't want to see the wonder and curiosity burning behind his eyes whenever he looked at me.

"I don't know if you'll be replaced, but yes, I have more than two mates." My attempt at bravery epically failed as my eyes brimmed with tears.

It was the truth. I had no idea how any of it worked. Would he be replaced, or would there always be an empty place in my heart where he should have been?

He pulled in a shaky breath and bit the inside of his cheek, nodding to himself. "I'll make an excuse to stay away from the revelry," he said abruptly.

He closed the distance between us and took my face in his hands, swiping at my tears with gentle fingers.

"You were always good enough, Lyra. I'm sorry I made you believe you weren't." He inhaled sharply as he tightened his grip. Then he leaned forward and kissed my forehead. "You'll always be the one that got away, and I've never been more sorry for anything in my life. I hope you find someone worthy of you," he whispered against my skin.

After a moment, he released me and darted out the door, leaving me alone with my broken heart.

Chapter Twenty-Four

"You are so beautiful," Vale whispered against my lips. "I want to kiss you so badly."

"Back off, Sasquatch. We spent hours on hair and makeup. You can kiss her after the revelry," Callie snarked.

"Feisty. If we don't find mates tonight, I'm bending you over my knee," Jed stage-whispered, and she squealed and batted at his chest.

"That's weird and hot. Quit confusing me," she snickered.

Vale was still hovering over me, and his lips lifted with a quiet laugh. "Have I told you how much joy you've brought into my life?"

"Not for a few days." I kissed his bottom lip and ignored Callie's complaints about smudging.

"You're the single greatest thing that's ever happened to me, Lyra," he said, wrapping me in a tender hug. "Whatever happens tonight, my sweet mate, you will always have me. Yesterday, today, and forever."

"Vale, I—"

"Don't make her cry, you dingus!" Callie interrupted. "Lipstick, I can fix. Smeared eyeliner and mascara are another story."

Vale shot her a look. "You literally wrote a spell for this."

"Yeah, but I'd have to say it again and do the thing with my hand. Bibbidi bobbity and all that. It's just easier if you keep it in your pants." She gave him the sweetest smile I'd ever seen and fluttered her lashes.

"We'll behave." I patted his chest as I admired him again.

Vale wore an elegant navy blue three-piece suit with a black tie and cuff links. On his left side was a lapel chain that represented his mated status. The pin displayed the phase of the moon on the night we'd met, and the pocket attachment was a star. Eventually, the star would be replaced by our bond's crest.

"You keep looking at me like that, Princess, and we won't make it to the—"

"Time to go." Puck leaned his head into the room. "We got the all-clear."

Even though Axel had claimed he wasn't coming to the revelry, my family had sent watchers to keep tabs on him, just in case.

I smiled up at Vale. "Hold on to that thought for later."

"You know I will." He kissed my knuckles and led me toward the door.

My brothers and parents would be announced after the guests arrived. We obviously couldn't go with them, so we had time to enjoy the festivities before the ritual began.

Since Vale and I had met outside of a mating revelry, I was excited to experience the ceremony with him.

We passed through the portal and entered a private room in the Winter Realm. The corridor had been cleared for our arrival. After we maneuvered through the empty halls, we finally reached the main entrance and blended in with the other arriving guests.

The Winter Court made good on their name, and walking into the ballroom was like entering a magical snowstorm.

The dark ceiling was covered with twinkling lights, and the floor was spelled to look crystalline, mirroring the image and making it seem as though you were walking among the stars. Frozen sculptures, lanterns, and shimmering chandeliers decorated the room, and white trees with leaves made of snowflakes towered over the dance floor.

Music thumped through the air, and floating fairy lights strobed to the beat. We danced, ate, drank sparkling wine from the ice fountain, and danced some more. Vale spun me around the room in a formal waltz, true to his upbringing, and ground against me when the beat dropped.

It was a perfectly magical night, and if I left without another mate, I would have nothing to complain about.

A hush fell over the room as a voice announced my family, and after they danced, the High Priestess appeared.

Vale took my hand and gave me an encouraging smile. "Are you ready?"

I was nervous and excited, but I knew I could do anything with him by my side.

"Yes. Are you?"

"With you, I'm ready for everything."

The High Priestess called the room to attention as her acolytes filed in beside her. Each of them had prophetic magic and would someday hold titles or positions in court, depending on how their gifts developed. Perhaps one day, one of them may even take her place.

The guests gathered around the dance floor, and the unmated females lined up against one wall as the unmated males took position on the other. Mated couples stood across from the podium where the High Priestess presided over the room.

She lifted her hands and chanted, and soon, an aura of magic wove through the air. The magic swirled around us, plucking at the mating bond until it was visible. Once the glowing threads emerged, they swirled through the room, searching for a destined connection. The excited chatter intensified as males, females, and couples followed the mystical cords that led them to their mates.

I was entranced by the bond linking me to Vale. It was bright, thick, and beautiful as it pulsed between us. No other connections sparked to life, but I wasn't upset.

"I get to keep you all to myself." A glimmer of satisfaction lit his face as he ran his fingers down my cheek. "Are you okay with that?"

"More than okay." I leaned into him and looked out at the crowd.

Sucking in a breath, I watched as Callie and Jed walked hand in hand, following their bonds that flirted with each other but connected to a mated couple. "Vale."

"I see." He kissed my head as we watched the group unite.

The couple was bonded, but the female was also mated to Jed and Callie—just as the male was to Callie and Jed—while they themselves remained unpaired. It was surprising, though not unheard of. Callie and Jed's close relationship made more sense now. They weren't mates, but they were in the same bond.

"Looks like I drew the short stick." Brev sauntered over, shaking his head. Despite his words, he was clearly happy for our friends. "What are the odds?"

Vale chuckled. "The Mating Revelries are specifically designed for this, so pretty high, actually."

Brev tipped his head toward the podium. "I wonder how that's going to work."

I glanced over my shoulder to find Sidric standing in front of a beautiful female, who happened to be one of the High Priestess's protégés. She was petite, with feminine curves. Her pale lavender hair fell past her shoulders, framing her sharp features. Her movements were fluid, and she carried herself with a sense of purpose and determination, but there was a rebellious spark in her eye.

"They match," I whispered to Vale as I watched my former lover find his forever.

Vale grinned. "They do."

"He deserves to be happy." Tears gathered in my eyes.

"Do you wish—" Vale started, but I shook my head, cutting him off.

"No, not in that way." I stood on my toes to give him a kiss.

He quirked a brow. "But?"

"But it would have been so much easier if I'd met and matched with him instead of ... you know."

Vale's eyes softened as he smiled at me.

"He was good to me," I finished.

"Which is why I like him. And I'm not at all jealous, but I am grateful he found a mate of his own."

I laughed at his teasing, and when the music started again, Vale and I made our way to the middle of the dance floor as the newly found mates disappeared to get to know each other.

Hours later, when my feet hurt but the party was still going strong, Vale and I slipped away.

"I'll be there in a minute," I told him as I entered the ladies' room. He nodded and joined my brothers, who were waiting for us to portal back to the castle.

After washing my hands, I splashed water on my face to cool down and patted it dry. We'd had enough champagne to flush my cheeks with color, plus all the dancing, but I felt like I'd run a mile. I was warm and my pulse was quick in my veins. When I finished, I walked down the corridor and pushed into the room where everyone was waiting.

But when I entered, I squeaked and stopped short.

My parents looked up from their conversation, and I noticed for the first time that they weren't alone.

My brothers and Vale hurried through the connecting door, looking as surprised as I was to see our parents accompanied by a single advisor.

Years of training kicked in, and I sank into a curtsy and bowed my head.

"Forgive me, Your Majesty. It seems I've taken a wrong turn," I said as I held my position.

"Rise, child." My mother spoke to me in her most formal tone.

The room froze—figuratively and literally. My breath fogged in the air before turning into tiny, delicate crystals. They sparkled like glitter in the sun before gently falling to the floor, where they gathered like frost on the carpet.

I tentatively lifted my head, unsure of what was happening. My eyes fixed on the man standing with my parents as my heart attempted to leap out of my chest.

He was tall, dark, and handsome—and he was staring right at me.

It shouldn't have been possible since the High Priestess wasn't present, but the mating bond surged out of my chest and stretched across the room to meet his. The two ends danced and twirled as they wound tightly around each other.

The male dropped whatever paperwork he held onto the table and marched toward me, eyes blazing with determination.

When he reached me, he wrapped one large hand around the base of my throat and tipped my head back to look up at him.

"Mate."

I whimpered at the claim but couldn't form the words to reply.

He didn't need them.

"I have been waiting for you for a decade, and I have grown weary in the darkness, longing for your presence. I surrender myself to you, entirely. Put me out of my misery and accept the bond," he all but demanded, staring down at me. "You are mine. I want you—now. Do you accept?"

"Yes."

The word was barely out of my mouth before he crushed his lips to mine. Wrapping his free hand around my lower back, he pulled me against him and held me in place as he took from me in a way I'd never experienced before.

And I loved every fucking second of it.

It was powerful and greedy. Harsh, yet soft. The kiss made my toes curl and my clit throb as I melted against him, ripe for the taking.

Amid that unconditional surrender, I felt the geas start to lift.

As the magic shifted, he pulled away to scan my face, his eyes alight with realization. His gaze intensified, then the corners of his lips curled into a knowing smirk. Without breaking eye contact, he dropped to one knee and watched with rapt attention as my true form was revealed to him.

Reader's Note

Thank you for reading Summer Knights Dream! Your support means the world, and I look forward to sharing the rest of Lyra's story with you.

For the latest updates and news, be sure to follow me on social media at www.ariadnebreylard.com

Happy reading!

Ariadne

Acknowledgements

I extend my deepest gratitude to my incredible husband. Your unwavering support and encouragement have been my anchor throughout this literary adventure. Your belief in me has been invaluable, and I truly couldn't be more grateful for the constant strength you've provided.

To my children, your patience and understanding during late nights and the writing process have not gone unnoticed. You are my greatest creation. I love you to the farthest star and all the way back—times infinity.

To my beta readers, thank you for pointing out insights and offering constructive feedback, helping me see what I couldn't. To my street team, your passion for the characters and the story is beyond appreciated.

To the fans, your unwavering enthusiasm has made this journey all the more rewarding.

To the talented artists and diligent editors whose expertise has elevated the quality of this book.

I am sincerely grateful for each one of you.

Thank you,

Ariadne

Night Kingdom

Queen Hesper Araphel

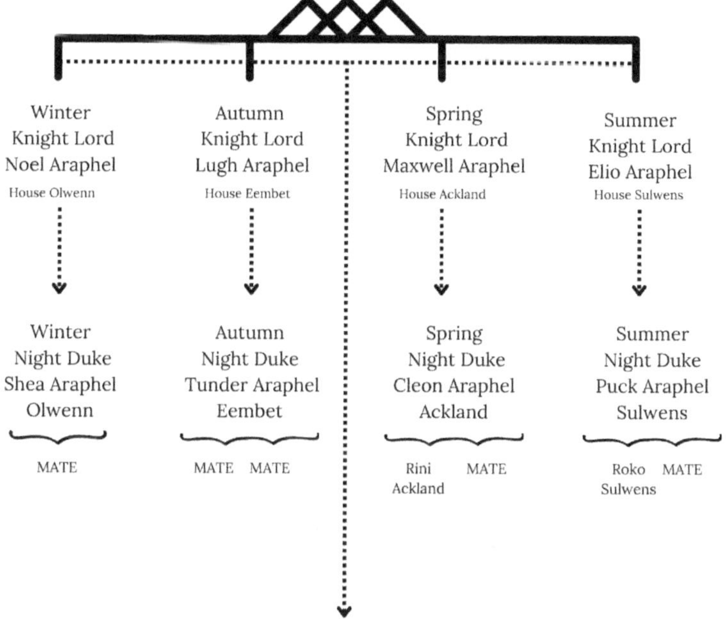

Princess Lyra Araphel

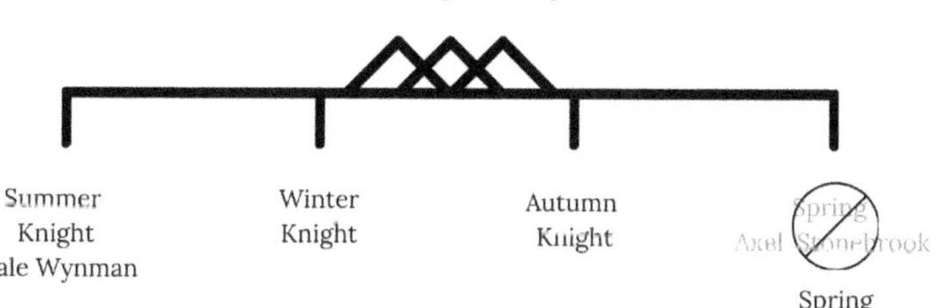

- Lyra (*Leer-uh*) — Night Princess of the Night Kingdom
- Vale Wynman (WIN-*mən*) — Lyra's Summer Mate, Noble Son of the Summer Court, Wynman House
- Mother — Hesper — Queen of the Night Kingdom
- Father — Noel (NoUL) — Knight Lord of the Night Kingdom, from Winter Court
- Pai — Elio (*Eh-lee-oh*) — Knight Lord of the Night Kingdom, from Summer Court
- Baba— Lugh (LOO) — Knight Lord of the Night Kingdom, from Autumn Court
- Papa— Maxwell — Knight Lord of the Night Kingdom, from Spring Court
- Puck — Lyra's older brother, Night Duke of the Night Kingdom, Summer, Elio's son
- Shea — Lyra's older brother, Night Duke of the Night Kingdom, Winter, Noel's son
- Tunder — Lyra's older brother, Night Duke of the Night Kingdom, Spring, Maxwell's son
- Cleon — Lyra's older brother, Night Duke of the Night Kingdom, Autumn, Lugh's son
- High Priestess — Prophetess of Fate, Knight Kingdom
- Axel Stonebrook — Spring Court noble, rejected Lyra
- Roko (*Rock-oh*) — Puck's mate
- Callie — Summer Court, Lyra's best friend
- Professor Atticus Warrock — Economics Professor
- Jana — Axel's girlfriend
- Meira — Jana's friend
- Jed — Callie's friend from prep school
- Brev — Callie's friend from prep school
- Sidric — Callie's friend from prep school, Lyra's friend with benefits
- Landor — Axel's friend who was at the Spring Equinox
- Chet — Vale's friend
- Paxon — Vale's friend
- Harlow — Vale's sister
- Clive — Harlow's mate
- Rogan (ROH-*gan*) — Harlow's mate
- Professor Ivy Rootsworth — Earth Elemental Professor
- Professor Reginald Copperplate — Accounting Professor
- Rini (REN-*ee*) — Cleon's mate
- Azael (AH-*zay-el*) — Axel's father, Spring Court Noble, Councilman Stonebrook
- Ranehall (RAYN-*hall*) — Night Court's Counsel, Noel's protege

About the Author

Ariadne Breylard is an author with a passion for crafting fantasy romance novels that are both sweet and spicy. She resides in a beautiful mountainous region, where the natural surroundings provide endless inspiration for her writing.

With an infectious imagination and a love for all things fantastical, Ariadne weaves tales of epic love stories, enchanting worlds, and mythical creatures that leave readers spellbound.

Her captivating writing style has gained her a dedicated following of readers and won the hearts of fans worldwide, putting her books at the top of Amazon Best Seller Lists.

When she's not writing, Ariadne can be found tending to her garden, filled with an array of vibrant flowers and plants. She also enjoys spending time with her family, beloved animals, and listening to the enchanting melodies of neoclassical compositions.

If you enjoyed Ariadne Breylard's writing, explore more worlds crafted under the author's other pen names.

www.ingramcontent.com/pod-product-compliance
Lightning Source LLC
LaVergne TN
LVHW010657110826
845149LV00014B/3128

* 9 7 8 1 9 6 3 3 3 6 0 2 3 *